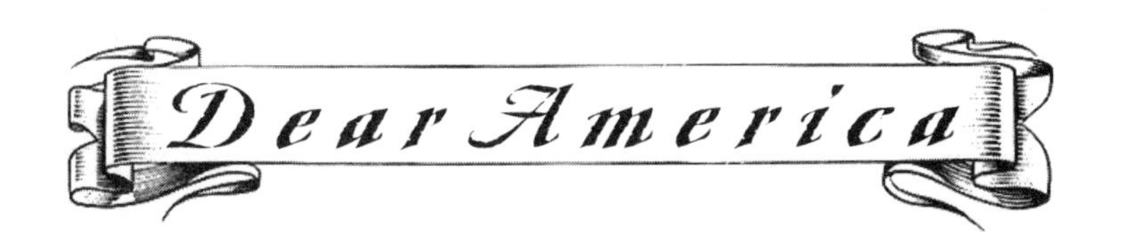

Love Thy Neighbor

The Tory Diary of Prudence Emerson

by Ann Turner

Scholastic Inc. New York

Green Marsh, Massachusetts

1774

October 2, 1774

Mama tells me that her wits must have wandered when she named me "Prudence." She tells me there never was and never will be anything prudent about me. When she says this, she always smiles to soften the words.

But I think 'tis true my name is not the right one. Abigail, my best friend, thinks my name should be Lively. I told her that sounds like a rabbit or a horse. My brother Walter told me my name should be Mouthful, because my mouth is always full of words.

Papa has no opinion, for he is far too worried to partake of such nonsense. Business at his store is going from bad to worse, and it is all because of these foolish politics. We are Tories, loyal to the king. Papa says God appoints kings to rule over his people and guard them from harm.

But many in our small village are Patriots, tired of King George's laws. They wish to govern themselves and do not like to trade with Tories, like my dear papa, who is so gentle, he could not even drown a rat in the stream behind our barn!

Papa says . . . here my quill sputtered. I must find out for myself what is happening in this strange and odd year of 1774. I will inquire. I shall ask questions. I shall listen at doorways. I will stand in shadows by pathways and listen to conversations. For I, Prudence Emerson, thirteen years of age, am no coward!

October 3, 1774

Here is how I came to have this wonderful book all to myself. It is small and narrow and used to belong to my uncle George, who died suddenly in his sleep three years ago. Since then my poor aunt has had to watch every shilling, and she only has one girl to help her, a little creature called Dorcas.

My thoughts run ahead of my words, as always. Aunt had been visiting and had picked up my slate from the Common School, where I go with my sister Verity and the other girls of our village. I should add, the village of Green Marsh in the Colony of Massachusetts in the year of our Lord, 1774.

Aunt gasped at my writing and said, "Prudence! Your handwriting is worse than chicken tracks in the dust!" Those were her exact words. Mama gave me a look, as if I might flare up like a badly trimmed candle. I know I should respect my elders, and so I bobbed a quick curtsy. It is a good thing to do when one does not know what to say.

A saucy girl would have said, "Thank you, Aunt, for making me feel small as a pea. Thank you, dear Aunt, for criticizing me once again."

Aunt told me of this accounts book that Uncle George had never used, and she ran back to her house to get it. When she handed it to me, she told me to practice my letters, and she would come and inspect it from time to time to see if I were improving. She is so unlike Mama, who is warm, smells of honey, and often smiles. Aunt's face is a stranger to smiles, and her comments are so needle-sharp that I have christened her "Madame Pinprick."

Madame Pinprick thinks I shall use these pages to improve my hand, but I shall use them to write down all the questions I have about:

Tories and Patriots, Papas who have different views (Abigail's papa is a Patriot), being the oldest girl in a family, growing up, wearing corsets, and having the misfortune to have curly red hair. I shall only write down what is in my heart.

October 4, 1774

This day I was minding my littlest sister Alice, fifteen months old, who walks and falls, bumps her bottom and cries, then smiles so that I smile back. I gave her a little rag and she pretended to help me scrub the kitchen floor. It is a thankless task. Kate sat on the settle humming to us, as always. She has been blind for two years, ever since a dreadful fever settled in her eyes when she was three. She is convinced that humming helps hens to lay, babies to sleep, and all to be cheerful.

In the midst of our work I heard a fierce squawking outside. Grabbing Alice and taking Kate's hand, we ran outside to find our rooster, Samuel, with wings spread and talons out, fighting a hawk!

The hens rushed around at the edge of the grass, making fearful noises and acting senseless. Jacob called to Papa to bring his gun, which Papa did. When he saw it was a fight between a hawk and our rooster, he lowered his rifle.

He told my brother that it was Samuel's battle, and we all watched, mouths agape. Kate begged me to tell her what was happening, and I did.

First the hawk pressed our rooster back, with its

flapping wings and open beak. Then Samuel rallied and pushed the hawk away. At our shouting and cheering, our neighbors, Mrs. Case and Emily, ran over to join us. Emily squealed, making it hard to hear the noise of the fighting birds.

After a mighty attack by Samuel, the hawk flew off, and Mama bathed the rooster's wounds with warm, salty water. I hope his wounds are not too deep. Mama invited our neighbors inside, offering them some bee balm tea. We dare not offer true tea to any Patriots now, for they refuse to drink it and consider it treasonous for anyone else to drink it.

What an exciting day this has been! I cannot wait to tell Abigail about it in school.

October 5, 1774

In Mrs. Hall's parlor, where Verity and I go for lessons (Jacob goes to the boys' school farther down the lane), I squeezed Abigail's hand when I sat beside her. I whispered the story of Samuel's ordeal, and she clapped her hands. "Oh, what a brave rooster, Pru!"

That annoyed our teacher, who is stout and bad-tempered, with protruding eyes. She made Abigail stand up and spell "anxiety," except spelling is not my friend's strength. She spelled it "angieety" and had to sit down and write it on her slate correctly.

I was sorry to get my friend in trouble, but does it not make a wonderful story? I love stories. I wrote "rooster, rooster, rooster" ten times on my slate and said a prayer for Samuel's swift recovery. He has been listless and slow since his famous battle.

October 7, 1774

Sad news today. Samuel, our rooster, died in the night. Jacob found him stretched out and stiff under the pine tree. Perhaps he had gone there to get cool or to seek relief from his wounds? It is with questions like that that I torture myself. My imagination is far too vivid, and I wish I could be calm and placid like my mama.

Papa comforted Jacob and said the trouble came from naming our animals. It was far better not to name them. But I cannot help that. Last year's pig was called "Skinny Benjamin," for he never quite filled out. This year's pig, soon to be butchered, I have christened "Fat Charles." I shall enjoy eating bacon from him when it is time, despite his name.

We did not eat Samuel but buried him instead. Papa

is such a kind father that he allowed us to do this. I made up a poem about Samuel's valor, which I recited over his grave under the big pine:

Bravest of roosters, protecting his hens,
Spurs at the ready, and wings to defend.
We miss you so sadly, you did not go gladly,
Samuel, the bravest of roosters.

The rhyming is a trifle off, but the sentiments are true.

October 8, 1774

Abigail came over to tat lace with me this morning, not a school day. As we sat by the window (for tatting requires much light and patience), we talked of her dog, who just had puppies, and of Molly Hawthorne, who has been flirting with Jake after church. I told Abigail that I did not understand how one flirted, and she replied that it involves tossing your head, batting your eyelashes, and smiling at the right time. I do not think I shall be very good at that. I might forget and roll my eyes and sneeze, or cough and get my hair in a tangle.

Then Abigail began to talk of politics, asking if we did not believe, as her papa did, that the colonies should form our own government? I was so startled that I dropped the horrid lace on the floor. But England helped pay for us to form these colonies, I said. And the king protects and governs us with his laws.

"They are wise laws," Mama called out from the kitchen. "Except I do not agree about the tea."

Abigail shook her head and took up her lace again. I fear I failed some sort of test, at least that is how it felt to me. Kate came out of the kitchen, her hands covered with flour, and flung her arms around Abigail. "Hello, Katie," my old friend said, and patted her head. They have been good friends forever.

There was a stiffness in the air as I tried to speak of other things, and Abigail claimed she was needed at home. At the door, she took my hand and said, "Oh, Pru, I do wish our papas thought the same way."

So do I, dear Abigail, so do I.

October 9, 1774

I seem to have more questions than answers. These are some that are flitting through my thoughts:

Is the king mad, as people say? Perhaps he is just angry at those radicals who tossed the tea chests into the harbor last year, all because of that tax they did not want to pay. A father would be angry, just as the king is.

What else will happen to us if we do not pay the money owed for the tea? General Gage and his soldiers have already taken over the port of Boston, at the king's command.

Why is not everyone a Tory? Is it not a good thing to be loyal to our king? It is how we have always been.

Why could I not have straight, golden hair, like Abigail's?

Later

As a seeker of knowledge and an answerer of questions, I stood in the dark room outside the kitchen tonight, listening to the conversation. Walter had just come in from chores, Papa was whittling something near the fire, and the others were cracking walnuts we found in the woods.

"Seth thinks this whole thing will blow over," Papa told my mother. I heard her saying that his brother was ever an optimistic man, and she did not know what would happen. There was a great deal of anger and mistrust between the Tories and the Patriots now.

As if to reassure himself, Papa repeated Seth's words. Walter said angrily that he just wished people would trade more with us, that it was not fair. Little Alice took up the word and marched around the room shouting, "Air, air, air!" The conversation ended in laughter, and I was happy to step out of the dark into the light of the kitchen.

October 11, 1774

Today I did not think of questions or listen at doorways. Instead I made marrowbone soup with my sisters in the kitchen. It is my favorite soup in the world.

Take one beef bone and sizzle it in lard in a hot iron pot over the fire.

Sizzle the onions beside the beef. The smell makes Kate jiggle her foot, for it is hard to wait.

Make Verity chop the parsnips and Kate the carrots, for she can use a knife if she does it slowly and carefully.

Pour two pitchers of water over the beef and vegetables, and let Verity toss in two pinches of dried thyme, salt, and peppercorns.

Afterward, Verity held her hand in front of Kate so

she could smell the spices. Kate sat on the bench, humming to make the soup taste fine.

October 13, 1774

I must be careful with this ink powder, for Papa has informed me he does not have an endless supply. The king should not have closed the port of Boston, he told me, fidgeting with his collar. He wondered how we merchants will survive when we cannot ship goods out of Boston or receive them. I think that sometimes he agrees with the king and Parliament, and at other times he does not. It is all very confusing.

I took Papa's newspaper up to my room to read when there was a quiet time in the afternoon, for I must answer some of my questions. The news was about the Patriots signing something called "The Suffolk Resolves," which declare that the people of our colony should not pay any taxes to the king, and they should form their own government. Papa says King George took away Massachusetts's right to have town meetings, but that was in punishment for dumping that foolish tea.

All I know is this: We have always been loyal to the king and shall remain so. Papa asks why should we change now? That would be like crossing the river in a boat and deciding halfway across to swim on the back of a horse. We are in the king's boat and will stay in it. I agree with him.

October 14, 1774

I shall just note here that Abigail and I went for a walk down by the river. I thought she seemed a little ill at ease, but still we talked and exclaimed at the sparkling sun, and my friend pointed out some geese riding on the waters below. They looked like small gray and white ships. Where were they going? Do geese ever have questions?

October 17, 1774

This day I stood in the shade of an oak tree near the inn. Two men went by with their heads close together talking of . . . ? Politics? Romance? Last Sunday's sermon? Mrs. Henshaw, wife of our miller, waited in front of the inn for the post rider to come. Her boy, Nathan, eight years old like my brother Jacob, kicked stones and picked the wings off orange butterflies. At that, I had to run out and hit his hand, which surprised him and his mama greatly. She scolded me, holding on to

Nathan so he should not hit me back, but I told her that any boy who picked the wings off butterflies should be sent home immediately.

"Your mouth runs away with you, Prudence!" Mrs. Henshaw exclaimed, and I had to go home because I was too angry to stay there. I know that Papa would not want me to get into arguments with any Patriots. And I knew that if I stayed there, I should pounce on that dreadful Nathan and bring him to the grass.

When I slammed into our house, Mama reproved me for the noise and asked what was wrong. I told her of Nathan's meanness, and she sighed. "Prudence, why can you not be prudent?" I must watch my words and be careful of my behavior, for Papa wants no one to have an excuse not to trade with him. Walter went off to see if there were any letters, while I had to spin thread as penance for my rash words. Spinning thread is penance indeed; it is even worse than embroidery. As I spun, I thought of some more questions.

Why do Mr. Strong and Mr. Pierce drink at the tavern?

Why do their legs wobble when they come out?

Why does Papa jump up and walk around the room after reading the newspaper?

What does Mama really think about Tories and Patriots?

Why is Walter looking so severe and distracted lately?

October 19, 1774

At school today, Molly Hawthorne (her nose runs), Emily Case (our silly neighbor), Alice Henshaw, and Hannah Williams (she is a sneak) all were sitting on one side of the parlor. They whispered busily when Verity and I came in, having to sit on the left side of the room with Charity Pratt, Mary Strong, Dolly Pierce, and Esther Parsons. All the Tories were together; all the Patriots were together.

Abigail came in late and looked flustered when she entered, shaking the rain from her cloak. She gave me an imploring glance, then turned her head toward the others. Molly waved to her to join them and, with a flaming face, she did so.

Charity patted my hand in a comforting way, yet I remember nothing of today's lessons; not one word, not one smidge, not one number.

October 20, 1774

I feel as grumpy as a sick cow. I cannot tell if it is because of what happened yesterday at school, or because of the amount of chores I must do. As the eldest girl in the family, here is a list of my work:

Wash clothes with Mama and Verity. I hate the feel of that slippery soap, and wringing wet clothes out in the cold breeze makes my hands stiff and red.

Spin thread for sewing. I detest sewing. It requires patience, and I have little of that.

Help Mama with little Alice in the morning. Sometimes I must change her nappies. I do not like that. When I fold the nappy about her, it is very difficult not to stick the straight pins into my sister's skin. Then she does howl!

Harvest herbs to help Mama with her midwifery and hang them in the barn. I like this.

Teach Kate her letters when I come home from school. She can recite the whole alphabet now.

Scrub the kitchen floor and help Mama knead and bake twenty loaves of bread each week.

I sound more like a complainer than a seeker right now.

October 21, 1774

Abigail did not shun me in school this day, yet she did not welcome me as heartily as she used to. I had forgotten to tell her about Samuel dying from his wounds, and when I did so, she gave me a sad smile and told me she was sorry. Then she turned and began chatting to Molly Hawthorne. Why does that girl not carry a handkerchief?

October 22, 1774

Mama commented on my long face today, and Verity and I told her about school, how the Patriots are all on one side, and we Tories are all on the other. Jacob said it was the same in the boys' school, and he was heartily sick of it. Mama sighed and pressed her back as she stood from stirring beef soup over the fire. Alice began to shriek, and over those shrieks I could only hear a few words of Mama's: "do . . . best . . . sorry . . . bear up . . ." I do not want to endure. I want things to be the way they used to be.

One cheerful thing did happen today. Walter ran into the house waving two letters from the post rider: one from Uncle Seth and one from his daughter, Betsy.

I have not seen my cousins, Betsy and Peter, in four years. If I remember, Betsy is small with golden curls, a tiny nose, and she likes to laugh. Peter is tall with my horrid red hair and a bump on his nose. He used to be a kind boy.

Papa read the news to us, all about those dreadful radicals, John Adams and John Hancock, who are helping to organize this rebellion in our colony. Papa fears they will lead us into war with Britain.

"I heard from Mr. Johnson that men in town are arming themselves, just as in other towns," Papa said. Mama sat suddenly on the settle next to the fire. Her voice shook as she answered that that sounded too much like war.

War. The word hung in the air like a black bird. Alice looked at me and said, "Pru-ee?" Her eyes looked frightened.

I lifted her up and took her outside to point to the geese flying overhead.

"They are going south, Alice, where there is no ice or cold."

"Ice-ee?" Alice put her arms around my neck. I wished for a moment that I could fly away with those geese to some country safe and warm.

Later

I am sitting in my cold bedroom with the candle flickering in the window drafts. Everyone else is downstairs, cracking nuts, roasting apples, and mulling cider. Even though it is chilly up here, I must have time to myself, which is difficult when you have five brothers and sisters. I shall copy my cousin's letter into this account book, to have a record of our correspondence.

October 17, 1774

Dearest Cousin,

I am in the midst of some fancy and difficult embroidery, making a white silk pocket to go with my best green dress. I am stitching a golden pineapple, for hospitality, as you know, and am happy with my work. Are you sewing or embroidering anything, Cousin?

Life is becoming very hard in Boston these days. Papa's temper, which has always been short, is tried often, now that our port is closed. He cannot stock his shelves or sell goods. When he went to open his store yesterday, there was a crowd of Patriots outside, shouting. They told him they would not trade with a known Tory any longer! Papa came home in a rage and kicked the water bucket. Mama was not pleased.

But enough of politics, dear Cousin. Is there any boy

whom you like or admire? In our church there is a nice boy called Edward, who is tall with a kind face and brown eyes.

Mama is sick with the boils, and Papa has been talking with men who are leaving our colony for England. I hope you do not leave, nor us. We were born here; this is our country, this is our home. But you could scarce believe how many Loyalists are fleeing to Boston now, for the protection of General Gage. I do feel safer these days with all the British soldiers to guard us. Except Papa says how can we possibly feed them all when we cannot import any goods? Life seems to be a constant worry to my poor papa.

Write soon, your affectionate cousin,
Betsy

Leaving! The word echoed inside like a church bell. If Uncle Seth was talking of going back to England, would Papa do the same?

I answered her immediately, before Verity came up to bed, for the candlelight disturbs her. Here is a copy.

October 22, 1774

Dear Cousin,

I thank you for your kind letter and news of your family. Truly, Uncle's troubles sound much like Papa's here in Green Marsh. The only difference is, my papa does not get in a temper. He just becomes very quiet and serious.

Dear Betsy, there is no boy whom I notice or who notices me. Perhaps it is because of my dreadfully curly red hair. Also, there are very few Tory boys of my own age.

I am happy your embroidery is going well, although I wish I could say the same for mine. Mama despairs of it, for my stitches unravel and I am too impatient. Verity is far better at stitching than I am and is working on her second sampler now. It has beautiful trees and flowers around the borders.

Papa has said nothing about leaving, thank God. I could not bear to leave, Betsy.

Your affectionate cousin, Prudence

Tomorrow Papa shall give a coin to the post rider to take our letters to Boston. He does hate to part with his money, but he hates even more not to hear from his brother. In three days, Betsy shall have my letter in her hand! Post riders are far faster than the stage wagons.

October 24, 1774

I asked two important questions this day. First I asked Papa if he thought about emigrating to England, the way some other Tories are already doing. He was bringing in an armload of wood at the time, and he paused for a moment on the doorstep. "No, Prudence," his words reassured me. "Not yet." Those words made my heart sink.

Then, as Walter was about to leave to help Papa, I asked if he thought Patriots could be friends with Tories? He paused and scratched his brown hair. It shifted his queue to the side. I think if I were a girl his age, I would find him handsome.

He sighed mightily and replied that he supposed so, but he was not finding it easy. He has lost friends over politics, and I thought for a moment he started to form the words, "Even Abigail . . ." Then he stopped himself, frowned, and strode outside.

Even Abigail, indeed. I must invite her over tomorrow. Perhaps if I try hard, this distance shall not open up between us.

October 25, 1774

Mama spread out some of her herbs on the counter in her stillroom, which is just off our kitchen. That is where she prepares her teas, oils, and unguents to help women give birth. She is such a fine midwife that she is much in demand. I heard one woman describe her, "Mrs. Emerson has kind hands, a soft manner, and the best medicine in town!"

Since Abigail has always liked pounding herbs, I asked if she'd like to help out after school was over. She hesitated when Molly called to her to come with them, but then she lifted her head and walked back with me, as she has so many times before. Mama was pleased to see her and begged her to sit and have a cup of tea. Abigail told us that her papa has forbidden them to drink it at home, but she missed it so that just this once she would. Mama smiled at her and gave her shoulder a little pat.

In the stillroom, Abigail crushed up pennyroyal while I chopped Seneca snake root. Steeped in hot water, both help mothers give birth. I saw my friend's arm slow, and one tear rolled slowly down her cheek.

"Why, Abigail!" I reached out to touch her hand. Then tears washed down her face and she turned her head away, murmuring, "Papa said . . ." But she could not continue. In a rush, she ran to Mama, gave her a quick hug and, sobbing loudly now, ran out the door.

It feels as if someone I love has died. Mama believes that Mr. Owens must have told her she can no longer visit us. I am hoping that Mama is wrong, that my friend is just upset. When I think of how much we used to do together! We would not only tat lace and knit by the window, we gathered spring greens down by the stream. We promised to be best companions until we were married or died, whichever came first. I even believed for a time that Walter was fond of Abigail, for she has a face like peaches and cream and a sweet disposition.

Tears make a poor ink, and I shall stop writing immediately.

October 26, 1774

It is true, what Mama said. In school today, Abigail did not even return my greeting. When we left Mrs. Hall's house, I asked if I had done anything to offend her. She choked out, "Papa says we Patriots must stick together," and ran away. Again.

I would not cry. I took a deep breath, grabbed Verity's hand, and marched home to tell Mama. She was very kind and made strong cups of tea to cheer us.

I fear it will take more than tea to do that.

October 27, 1774

I do not have the heart to write much in this journal today. I only note down that Aunt came for the inspection of the accounts book. There was no praise, only criticisms, and I fear the name I gave her, "Madame Pinprick," suits her. I shall only write that name on these pages (perhaps if I were *prudent,* I should only write down "M. P."), although I did tell Verity when we were in bed. She got to giggling, which made me laugh, and the mattress shook so that we just laughed the more. Mama had to stop outside our door to ask, "What is the matter, girls?" We could not tell her, and turned our giggles into coughs.

Laughter is the only cure for a sore heart.

November 2, 1774

It be a cold and dreary day. Ye heart is sunken like the millpond in summer. Ye thoughts are flying about like anxious hens. Ye spirits are poor and lowly. I only use the word "ye" because I think it funny; some of the older men in the village who wear big wigs in church sometimes use "ye." Abigail and I would tease each other, using that old-fashioned word.

Verity came and stood beside me as I wrote this. "Pru, your face is wet!" she said, as if I had spilled muck on the floor. I did not know I had cried.

Wiping my face on the sleeve of my dress, I told my sister I was going to bake molasses cookies. And I would take some over to Charity Pratt's house, as a gesture of friendship. For I am lonesome without Abigail.

Later

It takes so long to get the beehive oven warm enough for baking. But I did it, along with Verity and Jacob. He brought me pinecones and twigs to start the fire, Verity handed me the chopped kindling, and soon we had a merry fire blazing. We shut the tin-lined oven door and went outside to help flail corn in the barn. I thought it would be fun, and it was.

Verity, Jacob, and I hit the corncobs with wooden sticks, imagining that the dried cobs were Samuel Adams, John Adams, John Hancock, and Joseph Warren, all the men Papa told us were stirring up this revolution. We flailed that corn in a surprisingly short time and shoveled it into sacks.

Then Verity and I beat up the dough for molasses

cookies, letting Kate pour in the molasses and Alice press the dough on top of a cookie tin with her small hands. I swept out the coals and ashes into the pit, brushed the bricks with water, and set the cookies in to bake.

That sweet smell did much to lift my lowly spirits. I shall take them to Charity tomorrow, as I have too many chores to do so today.

November 3, 1774

Charity Pratt was so welcoming when Mama and I walked over with the molasses cookies in a basket. I do believe I would become most anybody's friend, excepting Hannah Williams, if they brought me cookies.

Mrs. Pratt bustled about the kitchen, inquiring if we would like some "white coffee," which, of course, we did. That is our secret name for tea. Mrs. Pratt wears dresses in the latest fashion, unlike Mama, but she is not affected or snobbish. I could hear her talking as Charity and I put on our cloaks to go walking. Mrs. Pratt spoke of friends who no longer spoke to her, of how Mr. Pratt had lost some business (he is a lawyer), and of how her husband had talked to men who were thinking of leaving the colony.

On the top step, Charity raised her chin and said that she would not mind leaving Green Marsh. It was too small. It was full of Patriots. And it did not feel safe, especially since there might be a war. My spirits sank back into my shoes again, and I could not talk.

I was so distracted that I set off for home without remembering to thank Mrs. Pratt for the tea. I even forgot Mama was still inside. All the way home my footsteps echoed on the hard dirt, *war, war, war.*

Later

During supper, my mouth finally came unstuck, and I asked Papa if he thought there would be a war in our colonies. He set down his spoon, wiped his mouth carefully, and replied that he did not know. He trusted that Britain would be able to contain this rebellion.

Walter reminded us that the colonists have already met in Philadelphia to talk about their relations with Britain. But he thought it a deal more than a rebellion, and that England might find the colonists a tough enemy in battle. Papa almost looked as if he were doing battle himself as he leaned forward and said that Britain had a trained army and seasoned commanders. That would be hard to beat!

I do not think Walter was convinced, and his hands clenched and unclenched on the table. Supper finished in silence, with only the sounds of the plates chinking as Verity and I washed them in the basin. Jacob threw the water outside the kitchen door, and I heard him whispering, "War!"

November 5, 1774

This day, Jacob and Walter loaded two sacks of dried corn in the wagon to take to the mill for grinding, for Mama needs cornmeal. I wished I could get out of the dark house with them, and suddenly, I could bear it no longer and pleaded with Mama to be allowed to go with them.

Mama took one look at my face, gave me permission, and as I flung my shawl about me, Kate begged to come, too. Outside by the wagon, Papa swung us up onto the front seat. Jacob rode in back on the sacks. A cold wind blew in our faces, and a few snowflakes drifted down.

Nat's hooves clopped on the hard road, and all the way Kate asked questions. "Have we passed the pond yet, Pru? Are there any ducks on it? Have we passed

Mr. Strong's house?" She has the entire village memorized in her mind.

When we stopped in front of the mill, Mr. Henshaw came out and stood in front with his arms folded. His black beard blew in the wind. He held up his hand and told Papa firmly not to come any farther, that he would not grind our corn.

Papa's face turned white, and Kate whispered, "What is wrong, Pru?" I had no answer for her. Mr. Henshaw went on to tell us that word had gone out through our colony: Patriots are not to help or assist Tories in any way. "I am sorry, Edward," he said.

"Not as sorry as I am, Nathaniel," Papa answered, turning the wagon and heading for home. Nat's hooves made a mournful sound on the road, and Kate asked no more questions. When I looked back at Jacob, I saw he had slid down among the sacks, as if he wished to hide himself.

At night

I had so many chores to do, I could not write more earlier. Mama was most upset when she heard what happened at the mill, and claimed that she would not help birth any *traitor* babies, either! Papa liked that and bussed her cheek, which made Jacob laugh.

I do not understand how a baby can be a traitor.

November 7, 1774

Mama brought out the mortar and pestle and set it down on the kitchen table. She asked Jacob to fill a bowl with the dried kernels from the barn. When he returned, snowflakes were scattered over his old brown coat. He lifted Kate up and put one of her fingers on the snowflakes.

She stuck out her tongue and licked the flakes from his jacket; luckily, there were enough so she didn't have to lick wool! That makes shivers go round my neck.

We all took turns pounding the pestle on the corn and dumping the ground bits into a bowl for Mama. "It is all the Patriots' fault!" Jacob sputtered. Kate took up the chant as she pounded, too, and finally Alice whirled around the floor, shouting, "Patey's, patey's!" and stomping her feet. That made Mama laugh.

November 10, 1774

Tonight there was a fight across the road at the tavern. Mama wishes we did not live opposite that place. I happened to be looking out the window and saw Mr. Pierce (poor Dolly's father) weaving out of the tavern door. Mr. Strong had his arm around him, and they were loudly singing about the "rebels" and how "Britain's forces would smash them flat!"

Some men followed them, and there was pushing and shoving. Papa wanted to run across and help them, but Mama grabbed his arm and begged him not to go.

"But a man must be able to help his friends, Martha!" Mama reminded him that those two men did not depend on the goodwill of others for their business, the way he did in the store. Papa puffed on his pipe a little, and then said that Mr. Pierce must learn to put a rein on his tongue.

Kate leaned against Papa and asked how could Mr. Pierce put a rein on his tongue? Would it not fall off?

November 12, 1774

Here is something new and surprising. There is a boy called Jeptha, thirteen years, who has just returned to the boys' school now the harvest is done. He is tall with red hair and has always seemed quiet and shy in church.

Jacob told me that today, when the Patriot children hissed and stomped on the floor when the Tory children recited, Jeptha came and sat beside my brother in school. And yet we know he, too, is a Patriot. Mr. Wood, the schoolmaster, had to rap his pointer to quiet the boys down.

When Jacob got out of school, Jeptha walked beside him. He nodded shyly to me and loped off down the street. Truly, not all *Patriots* are bad. I also am happy to see that someone else has been cursed with this horrible color of hair — red!

Here is another cheerful thing to keep in my thoughts: Thanksgiving is coming. That means stuffed turkey, baked squash, fresh apple pies, mulled cider, and rolls. My mouth is watering, and I must stop.

November 14, 1774

This was a dreadful day. Mama and I were scattering scraps for the chickens — they love pumpkin rinds, and it is the funniest thing to see the way they try to jump over one another to snatch up the best scraps — when we saw our neighbor, Mrs. Case, outside doing a washing. Mama and I greeted them and waved, but she seemed not to see us. Even when I called Emily's name, she turned her head away and walked back into her house.

"Come, Pru." Mama headed for the kitchen. Her mouth was grim and tight. I asked what was wrong with Mrs. Case and Emily, and she answered that this was happening all over the colony; that neighbors who used to greet one another do so no more.

Mama poured hot water from the kettle into a bucket and mixed it with vinegar. While Kate had to dust the furniture, Verity and I had to wash all the downstairs windows. Mama scrubbed the kitchen floor with lye and sand. When it was dry, she spread new sand and raked it with her broom into a beautiful swirling pattern.

"There!" she said. The sparkling windows and clean floor did much to make us forget our cold neighbors. Yet I still think kind words are finer than washed floors.

November 16, 1774

I am so tired that I feel like a rag doll. Mama has kept us washing, scrubbing, ironing, and cleaning every piece of furniture in the house. Papa smokes when he is angry. Unfortunately for us, Mama cleans house.

We had to do a big washing, with Jacob and Walter filling our huge pot with water after it had been set up over a fire. Mama and I put in the dirty clothes with soap and stirred them with long sticks. Then we must lift out the hot, wet clothing, rinse it in another kettle of water, wring them out, and lay them on bushes to dry. Alice's nappies we dry inside in the kitchen, so they shall be warm for her little bottom.

Verity fell asleep as soon as she sat on our bed, and I tucked her in under the blankets. Though I was tired, too, I must write in this journal and confess that I cried, a little, for my old friend, Abigail.

November 18, 1774

I woke last night to the rumble of wagon wheels outside our house. Verity started up in bed and grabbed my hand. "Who is it, Pru?"

I crept to the window and saw a man below, whom I could not recognize beneath his tricorne hat. I heard Mama hurrying down the stairs, the kitchen door slammed, and the man handed her up into the wagon. It is just someone come to fetch Mama for help with a birthing, I told my sister, and climbed back into bed.

This morning I had to get up early and start breakfast. Dear Verity helped by blowing on the coals to start the fire, while Jacob brought in kindling. We boiled water in a small pot and threw in four cupfuls of oatmeal to make porridge. I felt very grown up pouring out the strong tea into all our cups.

Papa smiled at us and said, "You girls have done a good job taking your mother's place." Walter tugged on the back of Verity's cap, which made her laugh. We are so lucky to have a kind Papa, unlike poor Dolly, whose father drinks at the tavern.

Later

Mama returned after supper, holding a pot of honey and a length of linsey-woolsey in payment for her services. She was happy that the birth was an easy one, Mrs. Johnson's third child. She is the wife of our blacksmith, and because he has been kind to us, Mama would never refuse to help his wife, even though they are Patriots. Only two days ago, Nat, our horse, threw a shoe. Mr. Johnson replaced it right away and said nothing to Papa about not doing business with Tories.

Mama hid her yawns behind her hand and went to

bed after a cup of bohea. Truly, we are fortunate that Mama is paid in goods; we need them in these lean times.

November 19, 1774

Charity sat beside me this day in school. She answered questions and appeared not to notice all the Patriot children on the other side of the room. I think I must take a lesson from her; I must keep calm and live up to my name. In that spirit I waved to Abigail as I left school, but did not wait to see if my wave was returned.

I am proud of myself this day. Except I find that pride does not make me any the less sad.

November 20, 1774

We woke early to ready ourselves for church. Mama had ironed all of our newly washed dresses, and they smelled so fresh and sweet. I laced up Verity's corsets, she laced up mine, and even Kate must wear them. I told Verity that I should prefer to slump and breathe rather than wear corsets to make me grow straight. "Shhh, don't let Mama hear you," she told me. For Mama firmly believes in the virtue of corsets, as does my aunt.

In church, we filed in and took our usual pew, not too close to the minister, for only the finest, richest folks sit there, but not too far to the back, for we are the "middling folk," neither rich nor poor.

Reverend Festus preached about the need for good relations with our neighbors. He told us that even though there are divisions within our community, yet we are still one village, still one people. One must "love thy neighbor."

Someone protested, "Not if they are Tories!" Mr. Johnson called out, "Hush!" Another reminded them that we were in church, and Mr. Festus brought his sermon to a hasty close.

Outside the doors, people gathered in groups, and I was dismayed to see that it was just like at our school, the Tory families together and the Patriots apart. I looked over at Abigail, who stood close to her parents. She kept her head down, as her father talked to some friends. Papa told us to come, and we walked quickly home. A cold wind blew, and it seemed to me that the wind was inside me, too. I could not get warm, even though Mama mulled hot cider, and Kate sat next to me on the settle and hummed.

How can I love my neighbor when my neighbor does not love *me*?

November 21, 1774

In spite of yesterday, we tried to cheer ourselves by getting ready for Thanksgiving. Oh, if ever we are in need of celebrations it is now! Verity and I brought up a basket of crisp apples from the cellar for making pies, although we don't bake those until the day before Thanksgiving. Kate and I polished our small store of silver — ten knives, six spoons, three serving spoons, a tea strainer, a butter dish, and some odd little piece that no one seems to know what it is for. The rest of our utensils are of pewter. Mama told me the silver came over on the boat with her mother and father, when they left England for a new life in the colonies. I can hardly imagine the bravery of my grandmother and grandfather, whom I never knew (they died before I was born).

Could I board a ship that tossed and bucked on an angry ocean for a life so far away? One would need a soldier's heart.

November 22, 1774

Papa and Walter took down their rifles from the rack in the stillroom and went hunting by the river. Jacob was allowed to go along, too. I wished I could go with them, not so that I could shoot anything, but just to be out of the house. At times I feel like a caged bird with all these people around and all the chores to do. Today I must sweep the dining room, iron the napkins, and ready things, for (dare I say it?) M. P. is coming to dinner!

Later

Papa, Walter, and Jacob came back, carrying the biggest, blackest Tom Turkey I have ever seen. I love that little red wattle that hangs from under its chin. I asked Mama if I might keep it, hoping it might bring me good luck, but she seemed to think that heathenish and superstitious and told me no. She said that prayer was much more likely to bring me good luck, and being careful, and watching my tongue, for my tongue has the habit of wagging more than it should.

Now Mama will dress the turkey (something I do not have the stomach for) and hang it for two days to improve its flavor. Jacob is going about the house making up a song about cooked turkey and stuffing and squash. Kate joins him, marching behind and keeping one hand on the back of his shirt.

She is not sad, she is not lonely; why cannot I be like Kate?

November 23, 1774

When I sat today to write in this journal, I saw my question from yesterday. It seemed like a twitch on the reins when driving a horse, and my mind galloped away with more questions:

Will we go to war against Britain?

Will Papa smile more soon?

Does Abigail miss me as much as I miss her?

How do you lift sad spirits? I know the answer to this: Make fresh apple pies!

Verity and I peeled and sliced the apples and set them in the pie dish, and Kate spread sugar over them. When Mama's head was turned, I stuck my finger in, pulled out two sugary slices, and popped one into my mouth and the other in Kate's. "Pru!" Verity reproved me, but then quickly ate a slice herself. Kate hummed all the louder after that treat.

Mama let Alice stand upon a stool and shake cinnamon over the apples. Alice crowed, "I help, I help!"

Today I feel lucky to have three sisters. I do not always feel so. I held my hand in the bake oven to see if it was hot enough for making pies, and it was. Verity counted out the time before I pulled my hand out, and it was ten, just right for baking.

When the pies were done, I carried them into the stillroom and set them upon the counter. I do pray that no mice find them during the night.

November 24, 1774

Before the sun rose in the sky, I helped Mama stuff our turkey with a sage-and-onion bread stuffing. Jacob filled the wood box, while Verity peeled and chopped a large orange squash to bake. Kate kneaded the dough for fresh rolls, while Mama and I stuck the iron spit through the turkey. Something fell into the fire and sizzled as we did that, and I jumped back with a yell. I do not like the insides of birds. Blood makes my stomach feel squeazy.

Thanksgiving was wonderful, even with M. P. as our guest. There were so many dishes on the table that I could scarce see our best white tablecloth beneath them. After Papa's grace, when he asked for the king's health and for peace in our colonies, we feasted on that delicious bird, chicken pie, squash, rolls, and stuffing. Aunt reminded us of the settlers who first came to these shores, and how they gave thanks for the food that kept them from starving. I noticed that my aunt had two slices of apple pie, while Walter and Papa had three each. She must have been very thankful. Yet Aunt raised her eyebrows at me when I took a second slice, reminding me that young girls should not be greedy. I did not answer.

Nothing could take away the joy of this day.

November 28, 1774

Here is a question I dare not ask my mama: Is she losing friends, too?

I notice that Mrs. Whittaker, who used to take tea with us before the troubles began, and who would sometimes come to knit by our fire, has not visited us in more than a month.

Are boys more unkind than girls? Jacob assures me that is so, although Verity argues that the girls at our school are just as mean as the boys at Jacob's.

When we went to join my brother at the end of lessons, two boys ran after him, throwing sticks and shouting, "Tory, Tory, Tory! You are on the wrong side!"

Jacob stood it for a while, then turned and growled that *we* are on the right side and they are on the wrong. Fat Harry and foolish Nathan (the same one who picks the wings off butterflies) jumped on my brother, and there was a very unequal fight until I joined in, jabbed my elbows into Nathan, and dragged Jacob away. Jeptha strode forward and took Harry by the arm, telling him that it was ungentlemanly for two to fight against one. I thanked him for his help.

I fear that I *like* being angry. I like the rush of heat into my cheeks and the feeling of strength pounding through my chest and arms. I am a most unworthy and ungrateful daughter. My skirt is torn and shall have to be mended so that Mama will not notice.

I am not living up to my name.

November 29, 1774

My candle blows in the wind coming through the cracks around the windows. My hands are so numb, I can scarcely write, much less make a neat mend in my dreadful skirt. I wish I were downstairs with the others, roasting apples, cracking nuts, and telling stories.

I detest mending almost as much as I hate politics.

November 30, 1774

This morning I poked my head out the kitchen door and looked up and down the road. Verity called to me, wondering what I was doing outside on such a chill and windy day. I could not say, "I am looking for Abigail." I have discovered that when someone goes away from you, your whole body feels empty.

December 1, 1774

Nothing of importance happened this day. I still hate school. I detest Hannah Williams, who sits next to my former best friend. Mrs. Hall scarcely calls on us Tory children anymore, as if our wits went a-begging. Jacob says he hates Nathan and would punch him, except there are more of *them* than there are of *us*. Verity never wishes to punch anyone.

December 2, 1774

We are almost at the end of the year 1774. It has not been a good year. I wonder what 1775 will bring? Such questions made me so fidgety and worried that I had to snuggle very close to Verity to go to sleep last night. The maple tree outside tapped its branches against the panes and it seemed they were saying, "Cold year, bad year, cold year, bad year." At times like this an active imagination is not a gift.

December 3, 1774

Since Aunt was coming for tea this day, I readied my diary for the "examination of handwriting." I even took one page and practiced all my letters, looping them up and making fine downward strokes.

When Aunt sat by the fire cradling a cup of tea in her hands, I set the diary in her lap, pointing to the practice page. The corners of her mouth twitched, and I believe she was pleased with me. She told me that she was certain now this exercise was helping, and was I not glad she had suggested it?

I assured her, fervently, that I was, for what should I do without my secret friend? I wish my aunt had a dear companion like this diary. Perhaps then her comments would not be so needle-sharp or her face so stern and unbending. After Aunt went home, Mama said that she really should come live with us, for it is not good to live all alone. Jacob had a coughing fit, while Verity and I shot each other such looks of horror that Mama had to reprimand us.

December 5, 1774

This was a happy day, for I had a letter from my cousin, and Papa has one from his brother. I did not have time to read until after supper. I read it now, my candle flickering in the cold draft. I know I am a foolish girl not to sit down in the warmth of the kitchen, but there is *everyone;* here, there is the blessing of just *me.* And it is not quite as cold as the other upstairs rooms, for the chimney is right by our wall and casts some warmth.

November 28, 1774

Dear Cousin,

Do you like to see our British soldiers dressed in bright red uniforms? I confess that the sight of a platoon of soldiers marching briskly along, their uniforms so gay and their rifles gleaming in the sun, cheers my heart.

Did I ever ask you if you preferred being called Pru or Prudence? I think I shall call you Pru, for it matches your red, curly hair. I wish to tell you, Cousin, that I do notice one soldier who keeps guard near the docks. I have never spoken to him, but have seen him when Papa takes me down to view the British ships. Please do not think me foolish, dear Cousin, but I have invented a name for him, Nicholas Gray Fielding. Somehow, it seems to fit him.

My soldier nods his head to Papa when we go by, for sometimes the troops know who are loyal to them. There is such a fuss about these politics, Pru. I am heartily sick of notices posted up, lists of names, and shouting in the streets. It makes my head ache! Papa is much more serious than he used to be, and cautions us to be careful. It is not in my nature to be careful.

Dear Pru, there is one other thing to write about, and that is the wonder of our church being decorated for Christmas. There are pine boughs spread about, and someone hung up a gold paper star. How that cheered Mama's heart, mine, and even my serious older brother's. Even though some think it "papist" to celebrate Christmas, I think we should bring that fine old custom back. Please write soon,

Affectionately, your cousin Betsy

When Verity called to me to come to bed, I sat for a moment, staring out the black window. I imagined the sweet scent of pine and the gold star gleaming in a dark church. Would it remind people of the light in the sky that led the wise men to Bethlehem? I wish I had a star to guide us to safety, to show us the way.

December 6, 1774

My dear sister is ill. She is Kate to me when healthy, but when sick she becomes Katie, what I called her when she was a babe. Some infection has worked its way into her cheeks; they are puffed out like pillows. Her eyes run, her nose drips, and she is feverish.

Mama told me to brew some sage tea for her fever, and I stripped the dry gray leaves off the bunch hanging in the kitchen. Those were the same leaves I harvested late last summer.

Verity threw the crackling sage into the kettle, and we sang hymns while it brewed. Verity's voice is clear and true, like a bird's; mine is hoarse and low, like a crow's. Walter joined in at the end, and his low tones made Katie smile.

When the tea was done, we put it outside on the step to cool. Even so, Katie tried to push it away, but Mama made her drink it. I soaked a woolen cloth in hot water and held it to my sister's cheeks, to bring down the swelling. She was most unhappy today.

December 7, 1774

I am praying that Katie has only a cold and fever. Papa brought down her truckle bed from their room and set it up by the fire. Mama hung a blanket from the ceiling to make a warm tent for my sister, and slept on a blanket nearby. I would like a tiny cough, so that I, too, could sleep near the warmth of the fire instead of in the dark at the head of the stairs. When the maple branches clack against the window, it makes me shiver. If she is awake, Verity grabs my hand and shivers, too. Then I must recite these lines to calm her: "I will lift up mine eyes unto the hills, from whence cometh my help." I do not tell Verity this, but I need some help from the hills, too.

December 8, 1774

Katie is no better this day. Her face flames red. I soak the compress and put it to my sister's cheek, but her fever is so high, she hates the hot cloth. Mama keeps fussing with Katie's bed, tucking in the blue and white cover, pushing the bed closer to the fire, then dragging it away.

Papa did not go to his store today, but stayed by my

sister, telling her stories of when he was young. Once she was asleep, he gave Mama a worried look.

"Edward, it is only a fever and swollen cheeks," Mama said. But, he protested, it was just such a fever that took away her sight two years ago. Mama shook her head and said it was not the same.

Papa was not reassured. He hates sickness and surprises, reminding us how quickly events can lead to disaster. He likes to be prepared at all times.

I pray God that he hold dear Katie in his arms and rock her gently from side to side this night.

December 9, 1774

My sister is no better.

December 10, 1774

She is worse. The fever flames her face. I can feel the heat from it when I stand nearby. Dear God, what will happen to her?

At night, Papa's heavy footsteps go back and forth, back and forth, as if by walking he might drive this infection away. Now Walter's steps are added to his, for he stays up with Papa most nights, keeping watch over

Katie. If ever she is thirsty, he holds her head and tips the cup to her lips. If she wakes the slightest bit, he sings to her. For Walter has a fine voice, and it would soothe me were I sick.

Aunt came today to see Katie and sat by her bed. My aunt reminded me of a large heron, with her bony knees poking up as she sat on the stool. She reached out one hand, drew it back, then patted Katie's shoulder. My sister did not open her eyes.

It is snowing outside. I can hear the flakes softly striking the glass of our windows. Perhaps it is a sign of hope?

December 11, 1774

Today Papa took us to church while Mama stayed at home with my sister. I found it hard to pay attention to the sermon, and stared instead at Mr. Festus's hands. They waved up and down, to the side, then out again. They seemed like small pink birds. I have no memory of his words at all.

Outside the door, Abigail hurried up to me, and for the first time in weeks, she actually spoke to me. She said she had heard Katie was ill, and was she any better today? I shook my head, saying that my sister was no better. Abigail reached out and gave my hand a little squeeze, which cheered me. Walter gave her a rather stiff nod, before we set off for home.

As we walked away, I turned to look, and saw her turning to look back at me, too. I wonder: When these difficult times are all over, could we be friends once again?

At night

When I sat by Katie, holding her hand and wishing I could think of something to help her, I had a sudden inspiration and spoke close by her ear.

"Did I tell you that Cousin Betsy's church is decorated with green pine boughs for Christmas? And they've hung a bright golden star that shines in the candlelight." Her head turned to the side, and encouraged, I told her that it would be like the star that guided the wise men to Bethlehem.

Her eyelids fluttered slightly when I stopped speaking, and I like to think she heard me. Then I had a second inspiration, as if a small voice spoke inside: Why cannot you put a star over your sister's bed to help her get well? I was so excited that I could scarce sit at the supper table, and instead searched the house for some gold paper. Mama wondered why I was dashing upstairs and down, but I dared not tell her. She would think me foolish.

When we went upstairs to bed, Verity asked if I thought Kate would get well. I said stoutly that of course she will be healthy again, and we both said a prayer for my sister's recovery. Besides, I told her, I have an idea, something to help Katie. But I did not tell her my secret yet.

December 13, 1774

While Verity and I were at our chores this morning, we heard a soft knock on the door. Abigail looked shyly in, pushing her cloak back from her hair. She wondered how Katie was faring, if she was any better? Verity cried out that she was very happy to see Abigail, and that we had been missing her.

Abigail blushed, greeted Verity, and walked past us to Katie's truckle bed, where she slept. My old friend always had a special feeling for my little sister and set down something by her pillow. Touching her hand, Abigail murmured a few words and turned, nodded to me, and hurried outside again.

When I went over to see what Abigail had left, I saw

an orange stuck with cloves on the pillow. It smelled of sun and cinnamon, and I couldn't wait for Katie to wake.

I stayed for a while, my nose pressed to the orange, until Mama came and set me to cooking soup.

Later

I went searching about the village today, trying to find what I need for my special gift for Katie. I have said my prayers; I have not snapped once at anyone, not even our fretful cows. I walked up and down our village streets, shivering in the cold, trying to think where to go. I have no money to buy this treasure. I thought of asking Charity, but I fear to ask for a favor from her.

In desperation, I knocked on my aunt's door and asked if she knew where I could find any gold paper, for sometimes on New Year's Day we give a present or two and celebrate the new year.

She put down her spectacles and told her servant girl, Dorcas, to go look in the attic in a small trunk there. She told me that some years ago Uncle George had given her some paper like that. Aunt was going to use it to decorate a handmade box.

Soon Dorcas appeared with a square of gold paper

in her hand. Aunt sighed and handed it reluctantly to me. I told her that it was for Kate, to cheer her up. Aunt twisted her hands in her lap and asked what good it would do my sister since she could not *see* it.

I was too shy to tell her that I thought the shining star might help heal Katie. Aunt cautioned me to let no Patriot see this star, as observing Christmas was *not* in favor in our colonies. It would be one more excuse to criticize us.

Summoning all my courage, I kissed Aunt on her dry and papery cheek and ran home, clutching the paper under my cloak.

December 14, 1774

Last night, as Verity and I sat side by side on our bed, I cut and snipped carefully until I had made a small golden star. "Oh, Pru!" Verity breathed, when I pushed some thread through a hole in the top and let it turn in the air.

Downstairs, I asked Mama to help me hang it above Katie's bed. She raised her eyebrows, almost said something (I think reprovingly), then stopped. I told her a star like this hung in Uncle Seth's church, so there could be no harm in it. An odd expression came over her face, and she said, "Christmas is a time of miracles, and we have need of one."

We got a nail from Papa's box and hammered it in the beam over Katie's bed. Her eyes flickered open at the thumping sound, then shut again. Mama and I fastened the star so it turned and gleamed in the warm air from the fire. I grabbed Mama's hand.

For one moment, the weary look went from her face, and she smiled. When Papa came in, he opened his mouth to protest, I believe, but somehow that star quiets people. Alice tried to climb on the truckle bed and reach it, but we would not let her. We all stood quietly, looking up at the bright shape.

If only Katie could see it!

December 15, 1774

I prayed this morning that Katie would wake soon so we could tell her about the star. Even though she cannot *see* it, I wondered if she could *feel* it. Perhaps she would feel a healing breeze from its five points as it turned in the air.

It was so cold at noon, we did not eat in the dining room but sat by the fire, crumbling our johnnycake with molasses poured over it and sipping cider. Suddenly, Walter jumped up and bent over Katie, calling her name.

Her eyes were open, and she reached up to take his hand. "Walter? Mama?" We crowded around her bed, and she asked for water. Both Jacob and Walter hurried to do her bidding, bumping into each other as they raced across the kitchen.

Perhaps the combination of our prayers, the scented orange, and the star are helping Katie, for did she not wake and ask for water?

December 16, 1774

The fever has broken! Papa and Walter have black circles under their eyes from staying up with my sister each night, and Mama is so exhausted she has gone to bed to sleep. Verity and I had to watch over Katie while Jacob kept little Alice from the fire.

Sometimes in the fall there are terrible, strong winds that come up the coast and blow across our colony, spilling haycocks, tumbling barns, and destroying crops. I feel as if one of those fierce winds has just flattened our house, and now we are peering outside, wondering if it is safe to come out.

Our Christmas star turns in the air above Katie's bed,

and when I looked into my sister's dark eyes tonight, I could see two tiny gold stars within. I thank God.

December 17, 1774

I am still so astonished that I can scarce write this down. It was three or four days ago that Abigail came to visit Katie, leaving that scented orange by her pillow. Today Abigail came back, looking worriedly in the kitchen door, inquiring after my sister. How I wished I could hug her and invite her in for tea, but instead I told her Katie's fever had broken, and she was better.

"Oh, that is good news!" Abigail's face brightened. She took something out of the basket hung from her arm and held it out. "Here is fresh bread for you, Mrs. Emerson, from my mama to you."

My mother wrapped her arms around Abigail as she thanked her again and again. After she left, Mama and I discussed whether Mrs. Owens was not such a fierce Patriot as her husband, for had she not sent that bread? It is all such a mystery to me.

December 18, 1774

We have been to church to thank God for saving my sister's life, while my aunt stayed at home to watch over Katie. For just this day, this Sunday, I felt that hostilities had ceased, as in some battle when the soldiers lay down their arms and call out to one another. There were no cold looks from our neighbors; there were no harsh words or a hissed "Tory!" as we walked past. Instead, our neighbors asked after Katie, and whether she was gaining strength. Jeptha came by and shyly asked after my sister. I thought of the courage it took for him to single us out. For one moment, it seemed we lived in a village where once again neighbors helped and looked out for one another.

December 20, 1774

All day Papa and Mama have been whispering together under the staircase like little children hiding secrets. I do not know what is in the wind, except Papa spent a long time in the barn with his carving tools, and Mama disappeared into her stillroom with her workbasket and her old yellow summer dress. Jacob informed me importantly that he thinks they are making something for Katie.

At supper, Papa smiled at us, set down his tankard of cider, and said, "You have all worked so hard and so well, and it has been such a worrying time, that it is now time for happiness."

"Hear, hear!" Jacob thumped his hand on the table.

I told Papa about Cousin Betsy's letter, how she had told me of the green decorations in their church for Christmas. Mama wondered if it might not cheer *our* hearts to put pine boughs about the house. Tapping his fingers upon the table, Papa worried that the Patriots might see it and criticize us, but Walter almost shouted that no Patriots came to visit us, *anyway,* so how could it harm us?

After the dishes were washed and put away in Mama's cupboard, we rushed outside to gather pine branches. Papa brought a lantern to light the way, while Walter stayed behind to watch over Katie.

As the light wavered over the snow and we called back and forth, I thought of the shepherds on the hills outside Bethlehem; how the light would have blazed in the sky, how the shepherds would have cried out to one another in surprise.

Inside, Jacob carried a candle while we put pine

boughs on the mantelpieces, on top of the mirror in the parlor, and over some windows. It smells like a forest, and I am sure the fresh scent will help my sister.

December 21, 1774

Katie tried to take a few steps this morning and almost fell. Walter carried her back to bed. Her poor face is so thin, and her hair has uncurled, truly it has. But the star gleams above her, and at bedtime she says, "Good night, star." Soon she will be well enough to get up, and Papa will move the bed back upstairs to their room.

Jacob, Verity, and I had a meeting today under the stairs. It is the only place in this house where one can have any privacy at all. I said that I had called the meeting to talk about Christmas, if we could not do more to celebrate it.

In the dim light, I could see Jacob's smile. He asked why we couldn't make presents for everybody, the way they did long ago in England. "Lavender! Lavender soap!" Verity cried out, and then shushed herself. For Mama, she whispered; we can put some of the herb in our everyday soap. Jacob thought he and Walter could carve something for Papa.

Without telling anyone, I decided to sew sweet-smelling sachets for my two sisters and fashion a yarn ball for Alice. I am so excited, I fear I shall not sleep tonight.

December 24, 1774

It was bitter cold today, with a hard wind blowing. I hid myself upstairs in our room, for Verity was below, watching Alice so that she should not get too near the fire, spill the water bucket, or do any of the things that she tries to do.

It was so cold, I had to keep warming my hands against my body so I could hold my needle. I sewed two ovals of printed rose material, stuffed them with lavender, and hid them under our bed. I could not help sighing, for when I harvested the lavender late last summer, our life was so very different! Abigail was still my friend, people traded in Papa's store, and Walter tied his queue neatly when my friend came to visit.

But I shall not let myself become downhearted. I have the two sweet sachets for my sisters, the scented soap Verity and I made for Mama, and a bag full of smooth river stones for Jacob to skip on the water. Walter and Papa shall each have a sharpened quill from me, while Papa is braiding a small whip to give to

Jacob. Mama finished Walter's gray mittens, and tonight we shall make Alice's present. Katie is up and about now, doing small tasks. She shall help me wrap the red yarn for Alice's ball.

Christmas bobs ahead of us like a bright moon in a dark sky.

Later

We were busy the rest of the day cooking for tomorrow; we made barley soup with a ham bone in it (from our pig, Charles), apple bread and scones, and two dried apple pies. The ham we shall boil tomorrow in water and cider. I can't wait.

Throughout the day I worried about what I could give my aunt, who is coming to dinner. Verity shrugged her shoulders, while Jacob made a joke that got us all to laughing so hard, we coughed. Mama asked what was so funny, but we dared not tell her. Here it is:

Jacob said I should make a slingshot for Aunt to hurl her barbed words at us!

Finally Katie tugged on my apron and said, "Why do you not ask *me,* Pru?" I put my hand in hers, and she told me to write a letter to Aunt, using my best penmanship.

I kissed her, asked Papa for some of his paper, and sat at the table to write something thoughtful and serious. After much trial and anxiety, here it is:

Dear Aunt,

I am most grateful to you for helping me with my penmanship, for I know how much I need improvement. I am a fortunate girl, indeed, to have someone who cares so much about good writing.

A fine hand is a protection against disaster.

A fine hand is a plea for understanding.

A fine hand will help with household accounts.

A fine hand shall persuade some man that his future wife cares about the proper things.

Thank you, Aunt, for your care,

Affectionately, your niece, Prudence Emerson

December 25, 1774

I am writing this upstairs in my windy room, holding pictures from today inside like candles to light the darkness. It is hard to believe this was the very first Christmas we ever celebrated.

Papa read the story of Christ's birth from the big black family Bible, and I held Alice on my lap. I love the thought of the infant Jesus lying in sweet-smelling hay in Bethlehem with the friendly animals all around. No one would have to remind them to love their neighbors!

We sat at the table with a sprig of greenery in the middle, and feasted on the food we had made. Jacob kept asking for more of the delicious ham. Somehow he pronounced "delicious" in a way that made Alice laugh. And this time, Aunt did not chide me when I asked for a second slice of apple pie.

A yawn just shook my hand, and I know Verity wishes me to help warm the bed for her. I shall finish my account tomorrow.

December 26, 1774

Jacob could scarce keep still after our meal, and he kept asking if it was not time to bring out the presents. Aunt repeated the word "Presents? Presents?" like an old woman with an ear trumpet who has not heard correctly.

Mama flushed and told Aunt we needed to celebrate in these hard times. M. P. put her hands on the table, and suddenly I felt sadness for her instead of anger. Her hands looked so thin and shriveled, as if they had never held happiness.

I gave my sachets to Verity and Katie, who sniffed

them and laughed. I handed the sharpened quill pen to Papa, who gave me a warm smile, while Verity presented the lavender scented soap in a small crock to Mama. She was quite surprised and pleased.

Jacob and Walter loved their gifts, and Alice danced about the kitchen and threw her yarn ball. Mama even had a small needle book for Aunt to keep her needles from tarnishing, and Aunt dabbed at her eyes when she held it. In a low voice she told Mama that she had nothing for her, but we all assured her it did not matter in the least.

Jacob gave a carved pipe holder to Papa, who was most pleased and immediately set his pipe in the groove. "This is very fine work, Jacob," he praised him.

Carefully, I laid my letter in Aunt's lap, and she picked it up, looking puzzled. Slowly, she read each line, flushing pink at the end. She bussed me on the cheek and told me she was pleased with my progress. A kiss from my aunt and praise!

Papa brought out something wrapped in a napkin from the cupboard and handed it to Katie. His face had the same secret, shining look my sister's has when she does all her chores with no help.

With careful fingers, my sister felt around the package, slowly unwrapped it, and lifted out a doll! She had beautifully carved wooden hands and feet, brown yarn hair, pokeberry juice eyes and mouth, and a soft cloth body. I recognized Mama's old yellow summer dress made into a doll-size one.

Katie hugged the doll and informed us that she would be called "Biddy, because she will do what I bid her." She touched the delicate hands and feet again and again, laughing at the feel of the soft woolen hair.

Papa had taken such trouble over Biddy. I felt the ridges between each finger, the tiny pointed fingernails, and saw that this was a doll for a blind child. Katie cannot see the body or face or mouth, but she can "see" the hands with her fingers.

At the end of this wonderful day, Papa carried Katie's truckle bed back upstairs again. Katie followed, clutching Biddy tight, and allowed Alice to hold one hand in hers. They arranged that Biddy should sleep between them this night.

December 27, 1774

My sister is so much better now that I can go back to calling her Kate. Though her legs are a bit wobbly and she tires easily, she is happy to be back with Mama and Papa in their room, sharing a bed with Alice. We have not taken down the gold star yet, and I shall not remind anyone of it. I think it brings us good luck.

December 29, 1774

Walter came home from helping Papa at the store, as he often does, but today his face was so grim and silent that it frightened me. When I asked him if any customers had come to the store, he replied that only the Widow Goodhue had sent for some buttons, ink powder, and pieces of foolscap paper. But that was all.

I summoned up my courage to ask if anything else was the matter. He sighed and told me he had passed Abigail out walking with Hannah Williams, and she had barely returned his greeting. "Once I thought . . ." He stopped, then thrust his hands through his hair. I know he was going to finish with, "to court Abigail."

Frowning mightily, he went off to the barn to feed the cows.

How I wish things were different! I wish we could step onto a magical sailing ship and head back to the time before angry words and distrust, back to the time when we truly did love our neighbors.

January 2, 1775

It is a new year. Will it be a good year? In some of the fancier houses in our town I know there are painted portraits of the family. I saw one once when helping Papa deliver some goods; there was a young boy in a swing with a dog at his feet, and his mother sitting on the grass beside. They looked happy and content.

If I were an artist, this is what I would paint: a lean-faced Jacob, an older brother with a frown that does not go away, a mother who looks too anxious, a papa who smiles rarely, and a sister who looks much like a frightened mouse. Only Kate and Alice are carefree.

January 4, 1775

With Katie being so ill, I have forgotten that I am an asker of questions and a seeker of answers. I stood behind the kitchen door today while Papa talked with Mama. The smoke from his pipe was so thick and strong that I almost choked.

He spoke of the *Boston Gazette,* published by the radicals, which Mr. Pierce showed him. "The weekly dung barge!" Papa snorted, and Mama laughed softly. The plans they have, he went on, and the lies they tell about the British soldiers!

In the darkness, I heard a sound at the window, something different from the tapping of a tree branch. Quietly, I went over and peered out. There were two shapes, one atop the other, looking in the lighted windows of our kitchen!

I ran to tell Papa, and he and Walter snatched up their cudgels and hurried outside. What looked like two boys ran down the street, and Papa shouted at them, but did not give chase.

"What were they doing?" Walter asked, once they came inside again.

"Most certainly it is just a boyish prank," Mama said, wiping the last dish. I hope she is right. I have my suspicions, however; one of the boys looked a deal like Nathan, for he wore the same brown coat and ran with that strange loping gait I have seen before.

At bedtime, I did not tell Verity I thought we were being spied upon. She frightens so easily, that it is a kindness to protect her.

January 5, 1775

We set off for school today, fortified with one of Mama's strong cups of tea. None of us wants to go anymore, but Papa wishes us to proceed as usual. When we took our places, Mrs. Hall almost pounced on Verity, asking her to recite the names of all the thirteen colonies. Standing, Verity sucked in a breath and began: "The names of the colonies are these: New Hampshire, Massachusetts, Rhode Island, Connecticut, Pennsylvania, New York, Delaware, Virginia," then she faltered and stopped. Her hands were shaking by her sides.

Mrs. Hall snapped at Verity to sit down, and she reminded us that true *Patriots* knew the names of all the colonies. Hannah Williams snickered, as did Molly Hawthorne, but I saw a sympathetic look on Abigail's face.

Anger made me bold and foolish, and I asked permission to speak. "Mrs. Hall, I did not realize it is an act of treason to be forgetful."

Then all the Patriots hissed and stamped their feet, making a fearful racket. I dared not look to see if Abigail was among them. Our schoolmistress said that I was dismissed for insolence and must go home. Holding my head up, I left and heard comforting sounds of the other Tory children following: Charity, Esther, Verity, Dolly, and Mary and the little sisters. Now what shall we do?

January 6, 1775

We did not go to school this day. After Mama heard our tale, she stood straighter and her eyes sparked. "Then I shall school you children at home. I can teach as well as some Patriot lady with more hair than wit!" Verity sighed with relief; Jacob shouted "Hooray!" and I was glad. Jacob's school is no better than ours, and Papa will be happy to have the help. I cannot help thinking that those sneaks who spied on us probably attend Jacob's school.

Mama worked us harder than a team of horses plowing a field. I had to line up the children in the cold dining room (Walter made a fire for us there, but the warmth did not reach the corners) and hear their lessons from the primer. Kate must spell some easy words, too, such as "cat," "Adam," and "fall." I was so proud when she spelled them perfectly.

Jacob was saucy and although he did not want to

practice his handwriting, he dared not be naughty with Mama. She set him to reading *Aesop's Fables* and told him she would quiz him later about the stories.

On our way to bed, Jacob said, "I thank you, Pru, for being saucy to that schoolmistress." He felt he had been delivered, and Verity agreed, singing under her breath all the way up the stairs.

January 8, 1775

Now we know what those boys were about, peeking in our windows and spying on us three days ago. In church today our minister preached a sermon about observing the customs of the colonies and casting off the customs of the past. Looking straight at our pew, he cautioned that no one must celebrate Christmas, that it was a "papist" custom and not to be tolerated in these free colonies.

Papa turned bright red, Walter paled, but we did not get up. My throat felt as if it were stuffed with wool when I thought of those two sneaks looking at our beautiful, bright star and the pine boughs.

We walked home quickly and did not talk to anyone. Once we were inside, Papa took down the gold star, while Jacob and Walter collected the pine boughs and threw them outside. I wrapped the star in paper and set it carefully in my small clothes' trunk.

Perhaps in the darkness of the trunk it will send out gold beams to help us.

January 9, 1775

Mrs. Pratt came for a visit today, along with Charity. She wished to join our little school, which Mama agreed to, but all the talk was of church yesterday.

"We are being spied upon!" Mrs. Pratt said, twisting her hands in her apron.

Charity thought it brave of us to celebrate that old holiday and only wished that her family had done the same. That cheered my heart a little, but we all miss the golden star turning in the warm air of the kitchen. Somehow it felt like a protection and a blessing.

January 10, 1775

In the middle of the night I sat up, sore afraid. Outside there was the clopping of hooves and raised voices. Verity woke and grabbed my arm. "Is it the Patriots?"

As I listened, I knew it was not the rebels but someone come to fetch Mama. I heard her telling Mr. Winters to calm himself, that his wife would be well.

I knew that she was swinging her red wool cloak over her shoulders, seizing her bag full of herbs and clean rags, and running outside to climb into the wagon. For Mr. Winters lives at the far end of town in a decrepit house. He and his family are Tories, so Mama did not have to decide whether she would help or not.

"I pray this birth goes well, Pru," Verity said, sighing. Poor Mrs. Winters, a gaunt and worn woman, has already birthed three dead babes.

The wind hurled sleet against the black window. I sat up in bed, straining for a sight of the wagon lantern, and was rewarded with a faint, flickering light that disappeared like a snuffed candle.

Why do babes always choose terrible nights to come into this world?

January 11, 1775

Mama has not returned yet. I had to take her place today, cooking meals and letting my sisters stir the johnnycake in the yellow clay bowl. Kate helped mix the batter with a wooden spoon, and I think that more of the batter went into my two sisters' mouths than into the black iron spider over the coals.

I fear the johnnycake was a little dried out when we finally took it out of the spider, for Kate had brought out her doll to play with. Alice patted Biddy's wooden hands while Kate felt for the doll's mouth and then held a teacup up to it. The rest of us helped make a soft bed for her in the corner of the kitchen and forgot to be careful about the cooking.

At dinner, Papa and Walter grimaced when they tasted the johnnycake, but at least I had a bowl of stewed pumpkin and strawberry preserves to go with it. Papa was quite gallant and did not complain, but Walter told me the chickens in the barn could cook better than this. Jacob snorted and said that their feet were not very good for mixing up batter.

I pressed my lips together and did not throw my napkin at Walter, though I was sore tempted. I am trying hard to bear up under hardships, the way Mama tells me I must.

January 12, 1775

Mama is back, and the house is the way it ought to be once again. Breakfast was tea, bread, and honey, and this day a load of cut wood from Mr. Winters arrived. Mama told Papa that she was quite surprised to receive several shillings from him for helping to birth his babe, but he was so happy to have a live son that Mama thought he would have given her anything she asked for.

Later in the day, I had time to answer Betsy's letter, which I received many weeks ago. I have been a poor excuse for a human being, as my aunt would say, and I am guilty.

January 12, 1775

Dear Cousin Betsy,

Please accept my heartfelt apologies for being so tardy in responding to your nice letter. It has been a busy time, and my sister Kate was quite ill with a high fever and infection. Your news about the gold star in your church and the green pine boughs saved us from melancholy and despair, Betsy. I managed to find some gold paper and fashioned a star to hang over Katie's truckle bed. This may sound superstitious, but I believe it helped her get well. Unfortunately, the Patriots found out about it (they spied upon us), and we had to take down the star and remove the pine boughs. I hope no ill will come of this.

Have you seen your soldier lately? You are lucky to have so many people to choose from in Boston. Here there are not very many Tories, and there are no boys I like who are my age. The only one who interests me is unfortunately a Patriot, Jeptha, but he has been kind to me and to Jacob. Please write soon, I treasure your letters.

Yours affectionately, Prudence

Nobody will ever be able to take Abigail's place, and there is not a day that goes by that I do not miss her. But it is a comfort to be writing to my cousin, Betsy, and to hear the news of our cousins and aunt and uncle.

January 14, 1775

Today Mama took me to see Mrs. Winter's babe. On the cold walk over (we did not take the horse and wagon, for our horse was lame), Mama explained, "It is time for you to learn about midwifery, Pru. It is good to have skills in dangerous times."

I was surprised, and said I thought I might be too young for midwifery, but Mama did not agree. She worries about Mrs. Winter, who is tired and gaunt. She is the kind of woman who might need a wet-nurse, in case her milk does not come in. I think that such an odd way of phrasing it, as if milk waited behind a door for it to open, and then marched in to take a seat.

When we reached Mr. Winter's house, there was a fire blazing on the hearth, and his wife looked up gratefully from her bed nearby. She is a plain, thin woman, with fretful fingers and two plaits of hair streaked with gray.

Mama asked how the babe was feeding, and Mr. Winters replied with a loud laugh, "He is a runt pig at the trough, always pushing his nose into the feed!"

To compare a baby to a pig was not very refined, I thought, and Mama's lips winced at his words. He went on to ask if it wasn't a good thing that his son, William, was such a good feeder, and wouldn't that mean . . . he faltered.

Mama reassured him that such a strong baby would live through almost anything.

Except war, the words came unbidden to my mind. I shivered suddenly, pulling my cloak about me.

January 16, 1775

Today Mama took me into her stillroom and showed me all the tinctures, ointments, and herbs she uses in birthing. She talked so long that my head whirled round like a spinning wheel. When I protested that I was too young to learn such things, she snapped that it was never too early to learn a trade. Her face was so pained and sad that I resolved not to disagree with her again. But her determination frightens me.

January 22, 1775

It was cold again today, with a strong wind blowing. Verity and I pulled on our stockings and two petticoats, laced up our horrid corsets, and stepped into our warm woolen dresses. Because today was church, I tied a blue ribbon around my neck. I confess that I hoped to see Jeptha there.

I also hoped that we should not have to endure any cold stares or unkind words. Papa says we must continue to attend church, for it would single us out even more should we not go.

We sat in our usual pew, with Mr. Pierce and Mr. Pratt nearby. Charity waved gaily before the sermon began. I did not see Jeptha, and thus my finery went to waste. The air in the church was freezing, in spite of our small warming oven filled with coals. I put Alice on my lap, wrapping my cloak about her.

I do not like Reverend Festus or his tired face and red nose. I like even less his high, reedy voice. When he began to preach, I was resting my chin on Alice's head, but I suddenly came to attention when Papa coughed. The reverend was railing against the king and his treatment of the colonies. He compared King George with an angry, dictatorial father who beats his children.

"Sir, you speak treason!" thundered Mr. Pratt, standing up. "He is our king, and we must be loyal to him. His troops will crush you if you do not —" The Patriots roared back at him, and Papa grabbed Mr. Pratt and hustled him out the church door, with the rest of the Tories following. Jacob hardly had time to snatch up the warming oven and run after.

Mama was holding Kate's arm, and Kate kept asking why we were leaving, and why people were shouting.

Papa replied that the minister was speaking treason, and we could not stay. It would be disloyal to do so. "Ebenezer, you must be more moderate," he told Mr. Pratt. Papa said he feared there would be reprisals if he did not keep his views to himself. Charity gave me a frightened glance and hurried down the street with her mama.

I am beginning to be as angry as Papa. Months ago I

sometimes wished Papa were more like the other fathers in our village, but I no longer wish that. *They* have shunned us; *they* have treated us unfairly; it is *they* who are stirring up trouble and who dumped all that tea in the harbor; *they* are the ones paying no taxes to our king, appointed by God to lead us; and it is *they* who will lead us into war.

January 23, 1775

Mama was in a strange state today. She started at the slightest sound, shied like a horse, sucked in a breath, and then tried to go about her work as if nothing had happened. Even Jacob noticed when Mama jumped up suddenly at a noise and spilled her tea.

"How clumsy I am!" she exclaimed.

Jacob looked frightened, and I put my hand on his arm. But I cannot change the angry atmosphere in our town; it invades our house, like black smoke seeping through the cracks. At times, I feel there is not enough air to breathe.

January 24, 1775

I am resolved to write of cheerful things. Kate knows the chickens by size, and she stroked one scrawny hen whom she has christened "Mistress Feathers." She says that "Mistress" needs extra grain and humming to gain strength.

What else is cheerful? Alice plays with her yarn ball, and best of all, Mama promises that soon she will teach her to go without her nappies, for she is old enough now. I shall be glad not to have to wash them!

Here is one other cheerful thing: We know one Patriot, Jeptha, who is kind to us. I shall practice his name here, for my J's are a dismal sight. *Jeptha, Jeptha, Jeptha.* I think they look fine, with all those loops and flourishes. If I cannot have a real soldier, like my cousin Betsy, I shall have a beautiful name in my journal.

Somehow that does not comfort me.

January 25, 1775

I went to Papa's store to get some more ink powder, and he gave me a sad look from under his dark eyebrows. "It is all gone, Prudence, and I know not when I shall get more. Do the best with what you have."

But I do not have any more, I told him. Mama says tonight that she can make ink by boiling up swamp maple bark in water. Tomorrow we shall go down to the edge of the fields to find some.

January 26, 1775

I write this with the last of my true ink. We peeled swamp maple bark at the edge of the boggy woods and brought it back home. Mama put some in a small kettle with water and boiled it and boiled it and boiled it. It looks like rusty water. Tomorrow we shall see if it can be used.

January 29, 1775

How could I have worried and fretted about ink? And yet, I am using it to write this entry, so I am grateful for that. The maple ink is a bit dim and watery, but it will have to do.

Late yesterday Papa ran into the house and seized his rifle. "Mr. Pratt's horse is stolen, and I must help find it!" Walter ran after him, carrying his rifle.

We had to sit and wait, reading from the primer and

telling our lessons to make the time pass. Jacob told the story of the clever fox from *Aesop's Fables*, I poked at the fire, Verity knitted, and Kate cuddled Biddy.

The grandfather clock bonged ten o'clock when Walter and Papa finally came home. They sat down without knocking the snow from their boots to tell us about Mr. Pratt's dog, and how he had led them to the stolen horse, hidden deep in the woods. The horse's flanks were covered with strange designs, and "Tory Nag" was written on one side, and a fist with a stick on the other.

"It is a warning," Papa said, "after that outburst in church. Ebenezer must be more careful." He feared worse things might happen to us Tories, such as being smoked out of one's house, like the man he had read about in the *Gazette*.

"Smoked?" Mama whispered.

They'd set fire to his house, and finally the poor man had to escape to the woods. Who could be so cruel? Did Mr. Henshaw have a part in stealing Mr. Pratt's horse? He is head of the Committee of Safety in town, the group that makes sure people obey the rules of the radicals from Boston. I detest them.

When we finally crept under our covers, Verity

could not stop shaking. She is a bundle of tremors, and it makes me so mad that I wish I had a rifle to shoot the enemy with!

February 1, 1775

As soon as my morning chores were done, I asked permission to go visit Charity. Mama pursed her lips, as she was putting a clean nappy on Alice. My little sister screamed suddenly, and Mama said, "There! I just stuck her with a pin," as if it were my fault.

After stirring the soup and taking the bread from the oven, she said I could go, but not to stay too long. Hastily, she wrapped a loaf of warm bread in a napkin and told me to keep it under my cloak. It kept me warm all the way down the snowy walk.

Charity answered the door and spoke gaily about the weather and wasn't it cold for this time of year, until suddenly her voice ran down, like an old clock. I handed her the fresh bread and told her we were so very sorry about the attack on her papa's horse. Mrs. Pratt seemed distracted, her cap askew. She kept picking up her embroidery, setting it down, dusting a small corner of the room, then whirling about to run to the door.

"Do not go walking this day, girls," she said in a shrill voice. Charity flushed and took me upstairs to her room. "Mama is still nervous," she explained.

Charity's room is far grander than mine, with a high-post bed and a canopy over the top. She even has a whole chest of drawers to herself. When I asked my friend if she did not feel like a prisoner in her own house, she tossed her head and said that there was no one she wished to associate with, except me.

We ate scones with unsweetened tea, for, of course, sugar is hard to come by now. I was anxious to see their poor horse for myself. Charity took me out to the barn, where a stout iron bolt had been fastened on the barn door. The horse seemed to have recovered from being stolen and painted, and munched his hay solemnly in the stall.

Charity said, "We had to wash him with a rag and soapy water!" Her lips trembled, and I took her hand. I had no words of comfort.

February 3, 1775

Another month has begun. My writing is no finer than it was at the beginning of this diary, or so Madame Pinprick tells me. She came for tea today and, taking out her spectacles, she sat in the best chair by the fire and asked to see my journal.

I looked at Mama, hoping that she would not make me fetch the diary, but she nodded to me, and I trudged upstairs and brought it down. Yet, at the same time, my heart surged with anger. To have my private thoughts so inspected! To have no place that I can call my own! If I had the money (which I do not), and the courage (which I do), I would find another account book and only write in that for M. P.'s inspection.

When I brought it down, I opened the book to the entry telling of the theft of Mr. Pratt's horse. She read it, making "hmmm" sounds, stopped tapping her fingers on the chair arm and sat, absorbed, in my account. When done, she clapped the diary shut, turned to me and said, "Prudence, it is clear you have no gift for handwriting, but you do have one for telling a story."

Here is a puzzle: Madame Pinprick actually complimented me on something. Somehow, I must find a way to protect my thoughts written down in this journal *from other eyes.*

February 6, 1775

Today I had to line up Verity, Jacob, and Kate at our table while they studied from Mama's primer. Verity read Kate's lesson out loud to her. Mama was roasting pork in the kitchen and making dried apple pie for dinner, but in between her chores, she hurried out of the kitchen to hear us recite. Alice insisted on standing in line with us and counting loudly as she tapped her foot; "one — free — two" was all she could manage, but I think she is the smartest little one in town.

Aunt came by and brought some slates and chalk with her. She set us to practicing our writing and praised Verity, chided Jacob for being slow and car less, and guided Kate's hand in making letters on a slate.

My sister was so excited to be writing that she could scarce keep still, and for the first time, I saw real tenderness in my aunt's face. She held Kate's hand, tracing the first straight line of an "A," then down and across. Mama always says there is some good in everyone. This must be the good that is in my aunt.

February 7, 1775

The seeker of answers has some more questions, and one is so pressing that I can scarce keep still. I am writing this alone so there is no chance Verity should see this.

Why would Walter be talking with Mr. Henshaw behind the tavern? (He is the head of the Committee of Safety, and Papa forbids us to speak with him.)

Why did it seem as if he did not want to be seen?

Is this an example of a wavering heart on Walter's part?

Perhaps he is not a Tory through and through. I must puzzle about this, without seeming to be a *sneak* like some of those Patriots have been. If anyone should wonder what I was doing behind the tavern, I was walking in the chill air to cleanse my lungs. Sometimes I feel so suffocated by this town, I must walk about or yell.

Later

All during supper (a stew made from a rabbit Walter shot yesterday), I snatched little glances at my older brother. How could he talk so comfortably with Papa when earlier today he had been with the enemy, a man who refused to help our father?

Though I am worried, I must not be hasty in imagining the worst of Walter.

February 10, 1775

I have not written for several days, for I have been too busy with chores, schoolwork, and fretting. Worry takes a great deal of energy and strength. I have been watching Walter carefully, to see if he behaves in any way *treasonous,* but I see no difference in him at all. At last we had a letter from Uncle Seth and one from my dear cousin.

When Papa read the letter from his brother, he jumped up and began to pace about the kitchen. Mama asked what was wrong, and he said there had been a meeting of the 2cnd Massachusetts Provincial Congress, led by that dreadful Patriot, Joseph Warren. They have decided that our colony should definitely prepare for war.

"But Edward," Mama asked, "were you not expecting this?"

Then they discussed, along with Walter, what would

happen if war broke out. Papa said we could emigrate to England, and Walter paled at that, protesting that we could not leave our store, our home, and our land. "Or," Papa continued, "we could go south or farther west, where they are friendlier to Tories." Mama let out a sigh and said she feared both and wished to stay here until the worst was over. Jacob voted to stay, as well, even though we all know it is Papa and Mama who will decide.

I felt so unsettled and wild inside that I had to leave the table. Verity followed me up to our room, saying she was afraid to stay downstairs and could she please, please read Cousin Betsy's letter, too. When she sat on the bed, her face was so white that I read out loud to her.

January 30, 1775

Dearest Cousin,

If you love me, do not speak to me of politics! I believe it is a disease, and I am sick of it. It is all Papa speaks of, it is all I ever hear. I wish someone would speak of balls, and parties, new dresses, sweet cakes, and a future with good things.

If I tell you something, will you promise to tell no one, Pru? I have had a meeting with Nicholas Gray

Fielding! You remember that is the name I invented for him. One day as I waited for Papa outside his store, my soldier stopped and spoke to me, touching his hand to his hat, and introducing himself as — you will find this hard to believe — Mr. Nicholas Spaulding of Surrey, England. Oh, such a fine hat it is, and such a fine man wearing it! He talked of Boston, of his home in England, where his mother and three sisters still live. I could tell he was homesick, and when Papa came out and closed the store, I asked if Mr. Spaulding could not share supper with us, and after some questioning of my soldier, Papa agreed.

At home I baked bread and made barley soup for supper, happy to have even barley to make soup with. It was such a festive time, to be together, to speak of something else beside the prospect of war. Papa questioned him closely about England, and whether he knew any Tories who had moved there. Mr. Spaulding said he had heard of many who had done so, but he was not acquainted with any.

My heart was in my mouth, Pru, at the idea of leaving home. How hard it would be! But do not be disturbed, for I am not in love with Mr. Spaulding. I just wish to think about something else besides men who are stirring up trouble, the difficulty of finding food, and what the future holds for us.

Write soon, your loving cousin, Betsy

I folded up the letter and put it in this diary. Verity's eyes were round as she repeated the words "my soldier." I cautioned my sister that she must never, ever repeat to Papa what was in this letter. Then I sighed, for I, too, wished to have someone special to think and dream about.

February 13, 1775

My maple bark ink is so pale that it makes it harder to write down the day's events. What happened today makes it even worse.

At the noon meal, Papa looked glum and worried, as did Walter. He told us that the Committee of Safety met in town last night to make plans for forming a militia. Mr. Pratt said that he heard there might be some test of loyalty of the townspeople, but that he did not quite know what it would be.

Mama set down her teacup with a rattle. "Well, that is not very helpful!" Papa told Walter to check on our horse and make sure the bolt was fastened securely on the barn.

When he returned, we all sat down to tea around the table, as Mama measured out the last of our sugar into the cups. Suddenly, there was a loud knocking on our door, and Henshaw entered, without being invited in, followed by our neighbor, Mr. Case, and the schoolmaster, Mr. Wood. They called out Papa's and Walter's names and told them that our village was forming a militia to help fight. "Will you sign this paper, Edward?" Mr. Henshaw waved a white square in the air. He told us that it was a promise that we would defend the colonies against Britain.

"Defend them I will indeed!" Papa said, springing out of his chair. "Defend them from this foul and treasonous plan! I will NOT sign your paper, Nathaniel." He opened the kitchen door and showed them out. Walter said not a word.

Mama's eyes were shining with pride, but her hands twisted in her apron. Verity and Jacob came in to lean against her, one on each side. It reminded me of calves in the spring pressing close to their dams. What will become of us?

February 14, 1775

After that frightening visit yesterday from the miller, the schoolmaster, and our neighbor, Verity and I tied on our nightcaps and climbed into bed. Mama came and stood beside us. "Do not fret, girls, all will be well.

God watches over us." She kissed us, once on each cheek, and left the room. Down the hall, I heard Jacob pleading with Walter to please come to bed with him and not to douse the candle.

Verity snuggled close and asked if I thought we would be safe. I could only hug her in return, for I did not know the answer.

February 15, 1775

Jacob called a meeting of the children under the stairs today. He said that it was up to us to arm ourselves and prepare for battle. His red hair stuck out in tufts when he said that, and his eyes were fierce.

"But what arms shall we use, Jacob?" I asked.

He showed us some sharpened sticks he had made and gave one to Verity, myself, even Kate. She seized one and brandished it. "I can fight, I can fight!"

My heart is heavy. I do not think that children with sharpened sticks shall be any match against grown men with weapons, but it helps my brother to be less fearful.

February 17, 1775

I am writing this a day later, for I could not write as it was happening.

Just before dawn, someone thumped on our door. I started and sat up in bed, while Verity began to tremble. I heard the sound of Mama's flint and striker in the bedroom beside ours, and her hasty steps on the stairs, followed by Papa's.

Slipping out of bed, I went halfway down the stairs, holding my stick, until I could see into the kitchen. A light slanted across the floor, and Papa exclaimed, "No, Martha, he's a Patriot!"

"I must," Mama replied, for Mrs. Hawthorne was having a difficult labor. Mama reminded him that she is Jeptha's mother, and he had been kind to us. She called to me to get ready and come with her.

For a moment, my feet seemed nailed to the stairs; then I hurried into our room, grabbed a cold dress from its peg on the wall, and pulled it over my head. All this time, Verity asked me questions:

"Where are you going, Pru? What are you going to do?"

I was not very patient, as I was asking myself the

very same questions. How could I help? What could I do?

Then a voice answered inside: *You know which herbs to brew to help the laboring mother. You can put pillows under her and care for the children of the house. Be of stout heart, Prudence, and be busy about helping your mama.*

When I reached the back door, Papa cautioned us to be careful and come straight home once the babe was delivered. Outside, a thin man in a blue coat and tricorne hat awaited us, holding his horses' heads. "Hurry, hurry!" he urged, telling us that no one must see him fetching a Tory midwife. Mama paused and inquired if there were some other midwife he would prefer. He fell silent, and we both climbed into the wagon, while he clucked to the horses.

I shall finish this tomorrow. The maple ink is becoming thick and cold. I am cold, too, and shall go to bed.

February 18, 1775

I must continue the story of the first birth I assisted at. When we alighted from the wagon outside the small house, my heart misgave me. What if I could not help Mama? What if it was dangerous to be here?

Inside, Mr. Hawthorne had set up a bed in the parlor, next to a blazing fire. Even so, I could see snow drifted across the floor, and Mama had to blow on her hands. I stayed outside while Mama examined Mrs. Hawthorne, and soon she told me to boil water and to put in some Seneca snake root. "She has been laboring this past day with nothing to show for it."

The father stood in the kitchen, fidgeting, while two younger children clung to his legs. I hung the pot of water over the hottest part of the fire, put in a root from Mama's bag, and attempted to comfort the young ones. All this time I wondered if Jeptha was awake yet.

When I asked if there was any food for the children, the father pointed silently to a crock on the table. The youngest girl, Ellen, had a thin face and an untidy dress. To cheer them, I told the story of the time our fat pig stole one of Mama's pies and ran away with it in his mouth.

By that time, the herbal brew was ready. I took some in a cup to Mrs. Hawthorne and held it to her mouth. The poor woman was exhausted, with sweaty hair and her hands clasping and unclasping the blanket's edge.

Mama said the brew would help bring the baby and not to be afraid, for she had never lost a mother yet. She did not say that of the babe, for sadly, even the best midwives, such as Mama, lose babies.

I shall finish writing this later, for I must go help care for Alice. She appears to be trying to roll her yarn ball into the fire and screams when Verity prevents her.

Later

We did not wait too long for that babe to make its presence known. The baby came with the rising of the sun, and with some fine yells from his mother. I was not in the room but stayed in the kitchen, amusing the children. At long last, Jeptha strode through the door, having been in the barn. Silently he held out a basket with six eggs, and I said I would scramble some for his mama and the children. Beaten with salt and pepper, the eggs cooked quickly in the iron spider at the edge of the fire.

When I brought the food in to Mama and Mrs. Hawthorne, I peeked at the baby. A small, red-faced infant was tucked beside his mother, and both looked exhausted. I looked proudly at the first babe I had helped bring into the world.

Jeptha took us home in the wagon, with Mama holding a small sack of oats in her lap and three skeins of gray wool as payment. She patted my hand, praised me for my help, and said that Papa should have new stockings.

When Jeptha swung me down from the wagon, he said quietly, "Be careful, Prudence. There is angry feeling in town." I could scarce thank him, and ran inside. Once again, I put on fear, as if it were a dreary cloak. How I *wish* that Jeptha were not a Patriot!

February 20, 1775

I have not seen Walter talking with Mr. Henshaw again, or with any other known Patriot in town. I have tried to watch him without actually spying, and I confess that suspecting my beloved older brother makes me feel guilty and shabby, like a thief stealing up behind someone.

But my doubts are not yet laid to rest, for today I was changing the bedding in his room and heard a crackling sound. Quickly, I drew out a folded newspaper, and I saw it was the *Boston Gazette,* the Patriots' newspaper!

I stuffed it back under the mattress, finished my chores, and hurried downstairs. My mind is whirling, and I know not what to think.

February 21, 1775

I am trying to push my worry aside and think of other things. To cheer my spirits, I sat and answered Betsy's letter.

February 21, 1775

Dear Cousin,

I share your hatred of politics. Things are getting worse in Green Marsh. Mr. Pratt's horse was stolen by the Patriots, hidden in the woods, and painted with strange designs and the words "Tory Nag." What sort of person would do that to an animal?

Sometimes I wonder if we should not be happier in Boston, much as I would hate to leave. I envy you the peace that General Gage has brought. I envy you all the British soldiers protecting the people of Boston.

My only other news is this: I helped Mama assist at the birth of Jeptha's little brother. Although new babies are not very pretty, I was proud to be there.

Please write soon. I treasure your letters,

Affectionately, Pru

February 22, 1775

Today I wrapped up a loaf of fresh bread for Mrs. Hawthorne when we went to visit her. Once we reached their house, the two younger children ran out and stayed close by me. I did not see Jeptha at all, even though I had gone to the trouble of combing my hair, tightening my corset strings, and sponging the soup stains out of my skirt.

I am happy to report that mother and "my baby" are well and healthy. Her milk has come in, and the babe nurses with great strength. I was allowed to watch him, with Mama, and my heart beat fast. Perhaps Mama is right to train me to be a midwife.

February 23, 1775

These past days have been gray and windy, and my spirits are low again. The air feels stifled and still. I wish to throw things against the walls. I wish to run screaming down the lane. I would like to slap Mrs. Case's face when she turns away from us. I would like to never attend church again — it is as painful as tight corsets. I do not wish to improve my handwriting, and I do not wish to grow up.

February 24, 1775

Again, my spirits are low. Perhaps I am sickening for something? Once I saw my life like a wide path stretched before me. I would walk along that path, making friends, marrying, having babes, and enjoying the beauty of this world.

But now that road is narrow and disappears into darkness. I am afraid to turn the corner, for fear of what I should find. It will not be happiness. It will not be safety.

Verity must have noticed my long face, for she has not called me to bed tonight as I write in my diary. She even said, "Take all the time you need, dear Pru." It helps to have a sister.

February 25, 1775

My fingers are trembling, and I know not if from anger or fear. Though it is late, I must write this down. Tonight, as we sat around the table eating, I thought there was a sound outside. Suddenly, the glass shattered, and a rock hurled onto our table and smashed the pumpkin bowl! Shards flew everywhere, and Mama jumped up with a cry. Blood ran down her cheek, and I rushed over to press my handkerchief to it. Papa leaped out of his chair, fetched his gun, and raced outside, with Walter right behind.

"Has it come to this?" Tears streaked Mama's cheeks. "It is not that I am hurt" — she waved my hand away — "but these are the people we knew, once our neighbors . . . now this!"

Verity and I swept up the glass, collected the clay pieces, and dumped them in the waste basket. Mama told Jacob to go out to the barn and fetch a cowhide Papa was saving for cobbling shoes. Seizing his sharpened stick, Jacob ran out to the barn and returned quickly. How much courage it took for him to go out there, alone in the darkness.

Mama and I stretched the cowhide over the broken window with the wind freezing our fingers while Jacob hammered nails into the window frame. Then we heard thumping sounds outside the kitchen, and Verity cried out. Mama reassured her that enemies would not come in that way. Papa and Walter entered the dining room, followed by Mr. Strong and Mr. Pratt.

"Our friends have come to protect us, Martha," Papa announced. The two men had rifles in hand. All four sat down, laying their weapons across their knees.

Mama hurried the rest of us upstairs and tucked us

into bed, for we should be in the way. I wished to be there with them, watching at the windows, defending our family.

I doubt I shall sleep this night, nor Verity.

February 26, 1775

This morning when we woke the men were gone. Mama made breakfast as usual, although there is a red gash on her right cheek. She wants no one to notice or fuss over her.

But she and Papa have decided that we shall not go to church this day! I have long yearned to cease going, for it is that uncomfortable, but somehow I am not relieved at all. It is too new, too strange.

Soon after breakfast, Aunt slammed into the house in a windy gust, hurled her gloves onto the table, and seized Mama in a great hug. "Martha, tell me it is not true!"

Mama's head poked over Aunt's shoulder, and I was amazed to see her eyes were wet. "It is, Emily." She told Aunt that they believed the rock was thrown to punish Papa for not signing that paper.

They continued to hold each other, rocking back and forth, both crying. "What will become of us?" my aunt whispered brokenly. And Mama did not, or could not, answer. That is what frightens me the most.

Aunt did not attend church either, and she slept on a blanket rolled up in front of the fire, for she did not wish to "abandon us to the enemy." I am a little uncertain how a thin, elderly lady could defend us, but I like her courage.

February 27, 1775

Papa brought home new panes of glass, after Aunt had gone home. Walter helped press the small pieces of tin into the window frame to hold the glass. His lips were so tight and grim that I dared not speak to him. Ever since the window was broken, he seems older and sterner. Perhaps I was mistaken in worrying about his loyalty.

When we sat down for our meal, Papa said a blessing over the stew Mama had made, thanking God for protecting us during the attack. I cannot help wondering: What will happen next? Will it be another broken window or something worse?

March 2, 1775

Mama cooks over the hearth, as usual; Walter helps Papa in the store, although they both took thick hickory sticks with them today. Alice plays on the cold floors and chases her ball, while Kate, Verity, and I work in the house, and Jacob tends the stock. But all is changed.

When I threw the dirty wash water out the kitchen door this morning, I looked up and down the icy street. There went Mr. Case in his blue coat; was it *you,* sir? There went Mrs. Whittaker in her green cloak; was it *you,* madam?

We will never know.

At night, I went over to the little chest and took out our Christmas star. It soothed me to hold it. I imagined the bright beams from the star piercing my skin and going into my soul, where they would give me courage. I have need of courage now.

March 4, 1775

It was snowing so hard when I went out to feed the chickens in the barn that I could scarce catch my breath. Snow piles up in front of the house, until it seems it will cover the panes. Wrapped in my shawl, I walk from window to window, staring into the drifting white.

When Mama poured hot water into our teapot this afternoon, her hand trembled so that water spurted out onto the table in a hissing stream. She ran to get a rag and gave me a guilty look. "I am sorry, Prudence. You pour this time."

Verity put her dress on backward this morning, while Jacob runs out five times a day to make certain the bolt is secure on the barn door. Kate carries Biddy with her everywhere she goes, even to the table, where she feeds her pretend scraps. Both Papa and Walter are quieter than usual. Walter no longer teases Verity or pulls on her cap to make her laugh. Although Papa has to conserve his tobacco, each night he still smokes so much that I expect to see a black smudge on the kitchen ceiling.

March 6, 1775

This ink is quite dreadful. I must find some ink powder or I shall have to open the window and give a great shout. We did not go to church this day, either.

March 8, 1775

Today is cold and windy, and the sun is far away. Papa's thoughts are far away, too. Now there are two deep lines on either side of my papa's mouth, and I know who put them there: the person or persons who hurled that rock through our kitchen window.

Mama had us line up for lessons again this morning. When Jacob protested that his time would be better spent defending us from the Patriots (he shook his sharpened stick), Mama set him to reading Proverbs in the Bible. She thinks that stopping our schooling would be giving in to the Patriots.

March 10, 1775

There was great excitement today, and a feeling of danger in the wind. Papa called a meeting of his friends to talk about the future, and how to defend ourselves. The men came in the back way, knocking the snow from their stout shoes and saying a quiet, "Good eve, to you, Mrs. Emerson." Mr. Pratt was there, Mr. Strong, Mr. Pierce, Mr. Hawks, and Mr. Phelps. I do not know any of them well, but I always see them in church, where we sit together. Walter was allowed to be part of this meeting, for at sixteen he is almost a man.

Mama made sure that Verity, Kate, Jacob, and Alice were in the kitchen, sorting beans by the fire. Kate can feel that the bad beans are shriveled. She said, "I can see with my fingers that they are not good for eating."

I held my breath, listening, for in the next room were six men and my brother, sitting around the table and smoking their long clay pipes. (Walter does not smoke a pipe yet.) Low voices came through the shut door.

Once, we heard a great thump and someone's voice raised in a shout. Alice began to cry. Then it became startlingly quiet.

Verity's eyes were wide and still, and Jacob stopped feeding the fire to turn and look at Mama. "It is all right, children, calm yourselves." But her hands pleated and unpleated her apron as Alice clung to her, and Mama did not pick her up.

March 11, 1775

I still wonder what those men were discussing last night. If they were drawing up plans for a defense, I cannot understand how they could do that. Out of a village of four hundred people, we number only sixty, including children. It is clear we are outnumbered.

When I asked Walter today what they had planned at the meeting, he ducked his head and said he could not tell me. Getting him to talk is like pulling prickers out of a dress.

If it were not for Alice's laughter and Kate's humming, I think we should all wear frowns.

March 15, 1775

My ink continues to be dreadful. These entries will be shorter until I remedy this. I shall note that Alice went a whole day without a nappy. Hurray!

March 17, 1775

The strangest thing happened this morning. Jacob and I had been in the barn, searching for eggs, and when we returned, we could see no farther than our hands. Kate and Verity had gone around to each and every window, pulling the shutters closed and closing the locks. The house was as dark as a night without a moon. Mama was upstairs, else she would have seen what the girls were doing.

Kate sat on the bench in front of the fire, holding her doll tightly to her chest. "Biddy said she is afraid of the Patriots, and I must protect her." Verity whispered that she only wished to help.

March 21, 1775

The post rider came bearing letters from Uncle Seth and Betsy. Papa said we already know the Patriots are arming themselves, and that there is no further news. He spoke of some letters written to the Tory papers by a man called "Massachusettensis" who exhibits great good sense. He thinks the colonies cannot survive on their own without the support of Britain, and that a way must be found to calm this situation. Papa and Uncle Seth agree.

Here is Betsy's letter:

March 16, 1775

Dear Cousin,

I wonder about the only boy you have mentioned, Jeptha, a Patriot. You should not think of him anymore, Pru. To do so will only cause you heartache and tears.

I am grateful that Nicholas is a Tory. I have hopes,

dear Cousin, I have hopes. I have prepared myself for marriage. I have a stack of hemmed linens; I know how to cook, polish pots, spin thread, and weave wool; I can knit a sock in one evening, embroider, and make teas for different ailments. I can play the pianoforte and dance a little. Is that not enough?

Dear Pru, I wish I could see you. Are you tall and slim like your father, or small and round like me?

Do write soon. I wish you would come to Boston and live with us until all is settled. I am certain you would feel safer here.

Your loving cousin, Betsy

I envy Betsy her hopes and her stack of hemmed linens. I fear I have neither hope nor linens. But more importantly, I had to rush down and speak to Papa as he answered Uncle Seth's letter.

"Dear Papa, will we ever move to Boston?" At first he did not answer me, but then he squeezed my hand and told me not to worry.

How can I not worry?

March 24, 1775

Now the chill wind is lessening, the snow is beginning to melt, and in some places I can even see the black earth showing through. The sun rises earlier in the morn, and sets later in the afternoon. It makes me think of a bit of lace being added on to the sleeve of a dress. That is the good news.

The bad news is that Papa was so quiet at supper that Mama finally asked him what was wrong. He never did tell us but went off into the cold parlor to smoke his pipe and read his paper. Perhaps he, too, sometimes longs to be alone, like me.

March 25, 1775

Mr. Strong needs a bridle on his mouth, for today he was forcibly thrown out of the tavern. We heard him shouting, "The British army will bring you to your knees! All of you! You have not the courage or training to fight them!"

Papa wished to go help him home, but Mama stopped him. She told him he must not endanger himself or his family to protect a man with such a violent tongue.

March 27, 1775

I do not understand how Papa and Mama make their decision, for today we did go to church. Perhaps they are afraid of stirring up too much bad feeling if we miss too many Sundays. I hated it. It was cold and chill and empty and windy, and only Tories came up to give us their greetings. This is not the life that I had imagined I would have.

March 28, 1775

While we were putting away dishes after supper, someone pounded on the door and Mr. Strong burst into the kitchen, followed by Mary, her brother Jeb, and Mrs. Strong.

Mama asked, "What is wrong?"

Mr. Strong held up a small dark ball with feathers stuck in it. Papa turned white, and Walter sat suddenly on the settle. "Tar and feathers," he whispered.

Papa had read accounts of such things in the Tory paper, and I suddenly felt sick. Patriots have been known to capture Tories, pour hot tar over them, and then roll them in feathers. They never recover and are left scarred and burned.

Mama comforted Mrs. Strong and told them all to stay the night with us. Papa went around locking all the shutters, and the men arranged a series of watches throughout the night. Jacob told them he would help with his sharpened stick.

How can our town ever come together again after such a thing? Abigail and I will never be friends again, I know this for certain, just as I know Walter will never be able to court her. We are enemies. We can never be neighbors.

March 29, 1775

In the morning we all slumped around the table, for none of us got much sleep during the night. Mary kicked and cried out, waking both Verity and me. Mama tried to make a breakfast from tea and scones, but no one ate very much.

Mr. Strong told us that he was moving his family to Britain. It was no longer safe to stay. They would pack only the necessities and take their wagon to Springfield. From there, they catch the stage wagon and go to Boston, where he will book passage for England. "If you are allowed to leave the harbor," Papa added.

When they left, Mary gave me a hug and waved a

mournful good-bye. Although she was never a close friend, she is still one of us.

March 31, 1775

Each time the snow melts from our roof and slides with a thump to the ground below, we all jump. Aunt came for tea this day and to discuss the warning ball of tar and feathers.

"It is worse, Sister," she whispered to Mama, as if we could not hear, as if we did not know. "It is these perfidious traitors." Her cup shook in its saucer.

When I asked Aunt what "perfidious" meant, she said it was "treacherous and disloyal." Here is a list of my words describing Patriots:

Perfidious
Disloyal
Traitorous
Evil and wicked
The muck out of stalls
The storm in our sky

April 3, 1775

I was a horrible girl today. I eavesdropped outside my parents' room after they had gone to bed. The reason I was being such a sneak is that something is in the wind. There has been talk behind closed doors. There have been conversations suddenly stopped when Jacob or I enter a room.

Outside their door, I heard a few low words: ". . . moving . . . Seth wishes . . ." Mama's voice, louder, ". . . not yet . . ."

Then Papa, ". . . your sister should . . ."

And Mama's reply, ". . . I will ask . . ."

Ask what? Sister should do what? I am becoming quite proficient at making question marks.

April 6, 1775

I should have expected this, after the overheard words three days past. The ink is sputtering as I write this: *Madame Pinprick has come to live with us!* Papa and Mama persuaded her that it was no longer safe to live alone in her widow's house.

She arrived in a blast of icy wind, as if God knew how much I dreaded her arrival. Papa and Walter brought in her small leather trunk and her sack of cooking pots. A few silver spoons from Uncle George were wrapped in cloth and buried in the floor of the cellar for safety. Her bed, which was knocked down for moving, is now set up in the parlor. Her girl, Dorcas, shall sleep on a straw mattress on the floor.

Tonight at supper, Aunt corrected my manners. She assured Jacob he did not know how to hold a spoon, chastised Verity for the way she sipped her cider, and cast a cloud of gloom over the table. The rest escaped her criticisms. I must remember to keep her in charity in my heart, but how I wish she had another relative far away, perhaps in the Colony of New York. They might wish Madame Pinprick to live in their household. Their manners would improve immeasurably, along with their handwriting. Pray God, I can keep my temper in check and my thoughts to myself.

There are only two good things from this move: Dorcas shall help us with the chores, and Aunt has given me a new bottle of ink to use.

April 7, 1775

I learned today that I have no knowledge whatsoever of household matters. I do not know how to mix bread dough. I do not know how to scrape sugar properly from a sugar cone. I know not how to determine if the beehive oven is hot enough for baking. I have no knowledge at all of how to sweep a floor the way a young girl should. Possibly, I do not know how to brew tea, either. Such were the comments from Aunt.

Later

Mama came into our room and sat upon our bed, one arm around me, the other circling Verity. I gave way to tears, and they soaked the front of my green dress.

"Do not lose heart, Pru," Mama said. She reminded me that we are all family, and we must learn to live together in such unsafe times. She told me I am a big girl, almost fourteen years, old enough to bear up under my aunt's words. "She is frightened, too," Mama chided me.

I am glad Mama came to comfort us, but she does not know what it is like to be me. I am a whirlwind of doubts and dark thoughts; I am a stream of sadness; I am a hurricane of rage.

April 11, 1775

I do not have the heart to continue so many entries in this journal. Aunt works us so hard, including Dorcas, and we are all so nervous and afraid that words seem petty and foolish. I shall note that I wrote a letter to my cousin, but I am too tired to copy it here. I told her about the attack on our house and the tar-and-feather ball given to Mr. Strong. Betsy wishes us to come live with them in Boston, and I am beginning to think it might be a good idea.

April 14, 1775

We took Alice and Kate for a walk today down the street. Papa said it would be all right, although we huddled together, looking over our shoulders. Jacob and Alice forgot and began to frolic and leap about like cows let out of a winter barn. I had to remind them to be quiet and careful, and the look on Alice's face made my heart squeeze in. How do you explain danger to such a young child?

April 15, 1775

Today Mama gave me a rest from my chores. She said my cheeks were becoming too thin, and that she did not like the worried look in my eyes. Little does she know about the fear in my heart.

Charity and I went down beside the river, with a gentle breeze blowing and the snow gone. Charity stood with the wind in her face, looking at the rushing water. "Sometimes I wish I could float on the river like a leaf," she said, "and the river would take me to a far-away place." I heartily agreed with her, but turned her thoughts from the future by searching for goose quills. I found three fine ones to bring home. All it will take is a little sharpening with Jacob's penknife. In such ways, I try to keep up my spirits.

April 18, 1775

I am writing less these days. Papa has met several times this week with his friends. They call themselves a "Mutual Defense League," and last night Mr. Pierce shouted, "Those Patriots will run like rabbits when brought to battle!"

Walter replied that the Patriots were better organized

than we think, and that they might fight fiercely for their cause. There was a sudden silence after those words, and I wonder if the men looked oddly at my brother. Was he giving an opinion or defending the Patriots?

April 22, 1775

I was in the front room spinning thread when I heard shouts from across the street. At the window I saw a post rider swinging off his lathered horse, shouting about battles. I raced across the street with Papa and Jacob. The post rider had ridden extra hard to bring news of battles in Lexington and Concord between the Patriots and British soldiers.

"The Redcoats went out to find our store of arms!" shouted the rider. "But we were ready for them, warned by Mr. Revere, and we shot and shot, from behind stone walls" — he ducked down and stuck out an imaginary rifle — "and we chased them all the way back to Boston!"

People cheered, and men threw their hats into the air. Ladies did the same with their caps. Papa herded us back to the house, with a grim and silent look, and told Mama what had happened. They talked and talked, along with Aunt, while the cows went unmilked, the eggs ungathered, my thread unspun, and the store closed. Papa said, ". . . may be time . . . ," but raised his eyebrows at me when I stood in the doorway.

I could not hear his plans. May God protect those poor soldiers! Papa said that many more were killed than Patriots. Mr. Pierce was wrong in his estimation of the Patriots. They *can* fight, and they *will.*

Later

Violence has happened, again. Around nine o'clock Mr. Pratt thumped on our kitchen door and rushed in.

"Edward, Walter, they are stoning Ethan Pierce's house. Will you help?"

Walter and Papa seized their rifles and ran after Mr. Pratt. I twisted my hands together, asking Mama if there wasn't something we could do, but she said all we could do was wait and try to be calm. Aunt protested that she did not want to wait, that she wished she could fight, too. Mama was so surprised that her eyes blinked and her mouth suddenly snapped shut.

How can I be calm? This is the worst part, this dreadful waiting.

April 23, 1775

By the time Walter and Papa returned last night, we were exhausted. The young ones were already a-bed and asleep. Mama made strong tea, laced with brandy, which they both drank down.

"There were fifteen or more, Martha, breaking windows and clapboards on his house."

Mama pressed her hands together. Walter added that all was confusion and darkness, for Mr. Pierce had bolted the shutters and kept only one candle burning. They had decided not to use their rifles, as it might have made the situation worse. Finally, the Patriots went home, leaving a badly frightened family and a house with broken windows and broken siding.

In bed, I cuddled close to Verity, already asleep. The grandfather clock bonged below, first twelve o'clock, then one o'clock, then two, as I imagined the scene at Mr. Pierce's house. What would I have done? I believe I would have grabbed a rifle, gone upstairs, and shot from a window. I still have not learned to be *prudent.*

April 25, 1775

If I wrote all day, I could not note down all that is happening. My head is whirling, and I hear Alice wailing downstairs. *Papa is going to move us to Boston!* He and Mama have decided; it is too dangerous to stay here anymore, and we will be safer under the protection of General Gage in Uncle Seth's house.

Those words are so bare on the page that writing them makes tears spring to my eyes. To not write at my little desk on the second floor, looking through the window to the far fields. To not work in Mama's stillroom filled with dried herbs and sweet oils. To not walk by the river with Charity . . . I cannot write anymore. My heart is weary.

April 26, 1775

I am snatching a small bit of time before supper to write about these events. We are busy all day and far into the night. Papa has the very devil driving him. We take only the most necessary goods, for we are allowed a mere fourteen pounds of luggage, and after that, one must pay four pence extra per pound. We are packing our clothes, Mama's medicines, and only some of Papa's tools. And this is why:

Walter is not coming with us, nor Aunt nor her girl, Dorcas.

Papa had read in a Tory paper about some Loyalist families, how their property was confiscated and kept by Patriots. But before fleeing to a safer place, a family might deed their farm to the eldest son, if he agreed to become a Patriot. Walter agreed to do this to keep the farm and store in our family's hands.

Papa and Walter have just come back from signing a promise that Walter will *not* defend Britain and that he wishes to be declared a Patriot. Mr. Henshaw, our miller, came as a witness for Walter. So now my old suspicions are stirred up again.

"The committee did not believe us at first," Papa said wearily at supper. "But Walter and Nathaniel finally persuaded them of this change in loyalty." He said he did not understand what Nathaniel had to do with all of this, and Walter ducked his head and tore his bread into small pieces.

Papa also told us that he had had to sign some papers to get a pass for us all to travel to Boston. He had to promise this time *not* to defend Britain, and to uphold the American cause. "Oh, Edward!" Mama cried.

"I am only protecting my family," Papa explained,

with a sad look. He said that now that we had this "certificate" we would be able to travel safely. For he feared there would be many soldiers near Boston.

I wonder if Walter protested about becoming a Patriot or not. I will never know. All I am certain of is this: We are leaving, he is staying.

April 27, 1775

I went to Charity's house to bid her good-bye. She looked so pale and worried that I scarce recognized my friend. She and her mother wish to flee to Boston, too, but Mr. Pratt insists on staying. He is convinced the British soldiers shall put down this rebellion speedily. I fear for my friend. Mrs. Pratt was most kind and gave me a beautifully embroidered handkerchief to take on our trip.

My sack is packed with three dresses, three chemises, stockings, two petticoats, two corsets (may they fall in a river on the way), handkerchiefs, this diary, and my golden star, wrapped carefully in paper. May it light our way. May it take us safely to Boston.

April 28, 1775

I have kissed the cows good-bye. I took one long last look at the barn loft, where some of Mama's herbs still hang. I looked out the windows and bade farewell to our fields. I followed Walter out to the barn and hugged him so long and hard that tears came to his eyes. And mine. He is my brother, after all, and that is what I think of now.

Then we began the sorry business of loading all of our belongings into our wagon. Papa, Mama, Alice, and Walter will sit in front, while the rest of us will ride in back among our sacks and a few crates. Jacob has made a nest of sacks to rest against with Kate. Aunt will stay at home, with Mr. Pratt to keep her company. Once we have reached our destination, Walter will drive the horse and wagon back home again.

I must go. Papa is calling me, and I must pack this ink bottle and this dear book into my sack. Good-bye, good-bye, I shall even kiss Aunt good-bye. I shall not blow a kiss to Mistress Case or Abigail or any of the others. Good-bye!

April 29, 1775

I am writing this at night, hurriedly, in a tiny and rather dirty inn. Walter drove us to Springfield, where we took the ferry over the Connecticut. Such a fine, wide, and shining river it is. I wished we were going by boat all the way to Boston, but Verity clutched Mama's hand and moaned during the crossing. Kate sniffed the wind and smiled all the way over, while Papa held Alice firmly in his arms. Kate informed us that Biddy "likes the sea." Jacob said that we had crossed a *river*, not the sea.

Then we caught the stage to Boston on the Upper Post Road. Is that not a lovely and dignified name for a road? However, the name does not match the way. It has holes filled with water. There are huge rocks jutting out along the sides. Sometimes we travel smoothly and almost rapidly, the four horses trotting along. Then we bump and jolt and shiver along.

There are three benches to sit on, and we take up most of them, with our sacks stowed beneath. Papa managed to stuff a whole bag of oats sewn up in tow cloth under his seat. It will be a present for Uncle Seth, and Jacob has been given the job of keeping watch over it. He still carries his sharpened stick, and he has a serious and sober look on his face when he guards the sack at our stopping places.

There is a couple traveling to Boston to visit their married daughter. They are quite silent, and the woman clutches onto the edge of her seat, looking rather green. Our driver, Mr. Phineas, is an extremely tiny man. Somehow he manages all those horses. I like it best when he blows on the horn to announce we are starting. It is such a gay, brave sound.

A yawn just shook my hand. I can hardly bear to write about saying good-bye to Walter, and how Mama sobbed and sobbed. He snatched Alice up for a last hug, squeezed Kate so tight that she squealed, kissed me and Jacob, and ran back to our wagon. I am sure he was crying, too.

April 30, 1775

If I wrote that we do not stop traveling until ten o'clock, who would believe me? If I wrote that Mr. Phineas warms his boots inside the wagon lantern, who would believe that? I hate to say that we are all sleeping, once again, in one small and dirty room. Papa and Jacob roll up in their cloaks by the fireplace, while Mama and we girls squeeze into the bed, with Alice and Kate in a nest of cloaks on the floor. Biddy, of course, sleeps in Kate's arms.

We had supper at the inn; beef soup (I could not find one shred of meat!), dry bread, and watery cider. Papa says we must not complain, that our main wish must be for a safe trip. I noticed he smoked a good deal after our poor meal.

Tomorrow I expect to wake at three o'clock, eat tasteless food, and set out upon the road to the blast of Mr. Phineas's horn.

May 1, 1775

This shall be our last night spent on the road. In spite of all the jolts and jumbles of the wagon, I rather like traveling. I like looking up at the sky and searching for birds. I like it when Mr. Phineas rolls up the canvas sides to let the breezes in. This was a pretty day, and tomorrow, we shall reach Boston! The married couple with the green-faced wife got off this morning, and did not even wave good-bye.

May 2, 1775

Thank God we are safely here in Uncle Seth's house. For a time, we feared we would not make it, for when we reached the outskirts of Boston, there were so many militiamen. They stopped the wagon and demanded to know who was inside. Papa got out and showed them our passes that testified we had passed "the test," as it is called.

Then one of the men — he had such a young face, with a thick black beard and blue eyes — waved us through. This is what frightened me, though: I thought he would *look* like an enemy, and he did not. He looked like someone Walter might go skating with on the millpond.

I shall write more tomorrow morning. My hand shakes with weariness.

May 3, 1775

Aunt Dolly is the kindest aunt imaginable, small and round and lively. She kissed us warmly when we arrived and showed us to our rooms, which are wide and gracious, with fine furniture. Betsy chattered the whole way, reminding me of my letters and the news I had given her. At the top step, she took me aside and whispered, "What has become of Jeptha?" I shook my head at her and followed my aunt into Betsy's room.

She and I will share a bed, and there is a smaller room at the head of the stairs, where Verity shall sleep with Kate. Alice is still little enough to bed with Mama and Papa, while Jacob sleeps with Cousin Peter, who seems to have lost the bump on his nose. There is one woman to help, Phyllis, and a boy called Guy.

This morning Aunt Dolly made us pancakes with sugar syrup, and a strong pot of tea. Uncle Seth, a short, round man with fierce blue eyes, took Papa off to see his store and explore Boston. Jacob and Cousin Peter went with them, while we settled in, unpacking our sacks and crates.

The air smells different. The sounds are so large and great! If I poke my head out the window, I can see a cart trundling along the road. There goes a priest walking; here come three women with shopping baskets, for the bell has rung to show the market is open (though Betsy says there is not much food for sale); and some British soldiers march past, their rifles shining in the sun.

"Oh, Pru, are they not handsome?" Betsy said. She is impatiently waiting for me now, and I must leave to go walking with her, Mama, Verity, and Aunt Dolly.

May 6, 1775

I can scarce find time to keep this journal, what with all we must see and do and what with the displeasure of my cousin, who finds writing tedious and recording in a diary strange. I find her a trifle bossy and am uncertain how to proceed. I shall have to snatch my moments when I can write.

This day Uncle Seth arranged to take us down to the wharves and see the British fleet. My heart fluttered with excitement when I saw the great ships riding at anchor with their flags fluttering. Uncle told us that some of the boats have almost fifty guns on them. Jacob's eyes widened at that, and he could hardly keep still. "I shall be a sailor," he announced proudly, "or a soldier." Uncle patted him on the shoulder.

It made me feel safe to see the British fleet and to know that it is here to protect us. We came home to the luxury of marrowbone soup. Somehow Aunt Dolly managed to procure it, and Phyllis has made a wonderful broth. She is a thin woman with lean hair, but is kind to Kate and Alice, so I am determined to like her.

The only other thing to note down about our new home is the noise at night. Mama, Verity, and I find it hard to sleep for the carts trundling, horses clopping, men shouting, and dogs barking. Jacob likes it and says it is much livelier than our little village. Indeed, Jacob.

May 8, 1775

I suddenly found myself in tears this morning, as I helped pour tea at the table. Mama said, "Why, Pru!" I could not answer her; I could not tell her that I remembered pouring tea for Walter and the special sigh he gave after his first sip. I could not say that I missed him pulling on Verity's cap, and swinging Kate up in a big hug. I must keep my spirits up. I shall not tell them how much I miss my desk at home, the smell of Mama's lavender soap, and the quiet all around. They think I have dyspepsia, a sick stomach, and Mama dosed me with chamomile tea. It did not help.

May 9, 1775

Uncle Seth and Papa had a smoking fest today after dinner. They like to sit in chairs near an open window and talk about politics. Uncle Seth said, "Brother, I do not like the way those battles in Lexington and Concord went. It is not a good sign."

Papa agreed with him, puffing on his pipe. They both wondered if war would be officially declared, and what would happen now that Boston was ringed with the American forces. "But Boston is full of British soldiers, and we have the navy," Papa declared. I wonder what Walter would have said.

The dickens! Just now, Cousin Betsy interrupted my writing, calling, "Pru, stop writing, and come out to the garden with me." So I shall. I am trying to "bear up," as Mama would advise me, and am trying to live up to my name. It is such a hard task.

May 13, 1775

My feet are tired from traipsing about Boston, and it is all so Betsy can find "her soldier." I guess that Cousin Peter knows nothing of her goal, for he seems happy to keep us company.

When we neared the harbor, she suddenly grabbed my arm and whispered, "There he is, Mr. Spaulding! Is he not splendid?"

I saw a lean man with a face almost hidden by his soldier's hat, and thought Betsy had exaggerated his good looks. Of course, I said nothing of this to her. He was busy marching and could not greet us, though I thought he sent Betsy a speaking glance. Verity, who walked beside me, mouthed the question, "her soldier?" We smiled at each other, enjoying our secret.

May 14, 1775

Today we received a letter from Walter. When Papa brought it inside, we saw the seal had been broken and the letter opened.

"Patriots!" Uncle Seth snapped. "Trying to get information," he said.

Papa sighed, then read the letter aloud to us.

May 9, 1775

My dear family,

I wish you to know that I am well, that the cows and chickens thrive, and that Aunt takes good care of me. I have not experienced any more of the Patriots' prejudice against Tories, although Mr. Pratt and Mr. Pierce barely return my greetings now.

On the other hand, Mr. and Mrs. Case now say hello to me. I had the satisfaction of having three customers in our depleted store. I shall have to order more goods.

Aunt sends her best wishes, hopes you are well, and wishes to remind Prudence to practice her handwriting. I, too, hope you are well. I miss all of you. Please kiss Biddy for me,

Your loving son, Walter

"Kiss Kate's doll?" Aunt Dolly exclaimed. "What a fanciful young man he is, to be sure, Martha!"

Mama hastened to explain that Walter liked to tease. Letters are a trouble and a blessing. They give us news of Walter and home, but my handkerchief was wet tonight.

May 19, 1775

The sun shines today, the water in the harbor sparkles and gleams, and one could almost imagine that Betsy and I were two carefree young girls, out for a stroll with Cousin Peter. He has started smoking a pipe, and imagines himself a very fine young man. I think he combs his whiskers as well.

As we walked along he told me that he wanted to enlist in a Tory regiment to fight the American forces, but there were few opportunities. He began to cough, and we had to stop while Betsy thumped his back. I do not think he can manage walking, talking, and smoking at the same time.

May 23, 1775

My spirits were low today, and Cousin Betsy kept asking me what was wrong until Aunt Dolly reproved her, saying, "Your cousin must miss home." I was so grateful to my dear aunt for being understanding.

Even Kate seemed somewhat downcast, and Betsy took her by the hand, leading her into their fancy parlor. It is such a grand room that it makes me feel shy, with its rich rug, heavy draperies, and shining pianoforte.

Cousin Betsy sat Kate beside her on the bench and began to play such lovely music. Over the tinkling notes she called out, "It is a piece by Handel." I do not know that man. But Kate tapped her foot, hummed, and a smile stayed on her face while the notes lasted.

Jacob had followed us into the parlor, and when the music began, he danced around on the rug, whirling an imaginary partner. I was happy to see a carefree look on his face.

May 26, 1775

There is a cloud of gloom hanging over the house today. The papers have come, and Uncle Seth and Papa are discussing the news. It is not good. Somewhere far to the north is Fort Ticonderoga. It was an important fort, Uncle said heavily, with many weapons, and it has fallen to the American army. A man called Benedict Arnold led a force and captured the fort. The paper said that the attack was so sudden and surprising that one of the British officers had no time to put his pants on!

Jacob laughed at that, and had to suddenly clamp his mouth shut at a fierce look from our papa.

Uncle fears that the American forces may have captured some of the British guns and cannons. That is not good news, for those weapons could be turned against us.

May 29, 1775

I thought that when we fled to Boston, life would somehow be easier. It is only by good luck and planning that Aunt Dolly and Uncle Seth have a store of food in their cellar. Unfortunately, it is mostly dried food, so we have pea soup, barley soup, porridge, and johnnycake. Sometimes Aunt Dolly manages to buy some fish, and then we have fried fish cakes to eat. Kate likes them, as do I.

Still, we are under the protection of General Gage, and that must count for something. I do not have to start out of my bed, imagining the worst. I do not have to be afraid of an attack on our house, or that Papa shall receive a horrible ball of tar and feathers.

I am beginning to get used to the noise, for I sleep better at night. And even if I wish for ham boiled in cider, I expect peace is better than a full stomach.

June 1, 1775

If I were back home, the onions, cabbages, and carrots would be up. I would tend them carefully, making sure nothing harmed the new seedlings. There is a bit of land behind Uncle Seth's house, and today we all worked on digging the ground, breaking up the clods of dirt, and readying it for planting. Aunt Dolly says she can get seeds from her neighbor. We must grow some of our own food.

While Mama was helping, she asked Aunt Dolly if she could let her friends know about Mama being a midwife. "Some income would be useful," Mama added, and Aunt agreed. She had a shrewd look in her eye; she has not been married to a shopkeeper for nothing all these years.

Today was Kate's sixth birthday. We did not do much to celebrate it, but Aunt Dolly made a sweet tart for dessert. Peter slipped half of his to Kate, for he has taken a fancy to her, as most do. Cousin Betsy played some more music by that man called Handel, and Papa and Mama waltzed around the parlor while Jacob twirled Kate. I looked on with Alice in my arms, and thought, this is *almost* a home, but not like what we left behind. I wonder what Walter is doing this night. I wonder how Aunt is treating him, and I do hope they are happy.

June 3, 1775

Mr. Spaulding came to supper this evening. There was never such a to-do throughout the house. Betsy dusted everything, she set their servant Phyllis to scrubbing the hall tiles, and Aunt Dolly had to make something special for supper.

I know not how she did it, but we had some mutton to eat. I believe that Uncle Seth has what they call "connections," which help somehow. Phyllis roasted the meat until the outside was crackling and the inside juicy. What a feast.

Mr. Spaulding looked as if he had suddenly been transported to paradise. "This is a fine meal, Mrs. Emerson," he complimented Aunt Dolly. I would not say he is a man of few words, but I would not say he is a man of many words, either. He makes up for that with a gentle and kind spirit, for he noticed Kate and did a little twirl around the parlor with her when Cousin Betsy played the pianoforte. He seemed most impressed with her rollicking music. Mr. Spaulding even held little Alice in his arms and danced with her. She was shy at first and kept her head turned away from him, but by the end of the dance she was laughing.

I could almost imagine that we are living an everyday life here. I could almost forget the British ships, riding in the harbor; the British soldiers, marching through Boston; and the militiamen, ringed around the edges.

But I cannot.

June 4, 1775

Today I felt proud to be a Tory. At supper, Uncle Seth lifted his glass (somehow he does not run out of port) and said, "A toast to King George, a toast." We all held up our glasses to the king, wishing him a happy birthday far across the sea. Kate asked, "Will he know we are wishing him a happy birthday? Can he hear us far away?"

Verity patted her back and answered that perhaps his spirit would know, or perhaps he would know in his dreams.

Papa wondered if a time would come when we would no longer lift a glass to King George. "Never!" Uncle exclaimed, but Mama asked what would happen if the militiamen beat the British forces and the Americans governed the colonies. Neither Uncle nor Papa answered her. Uncle took a deep swig of his port and sighed.

I cannot imagine that. It would be like a man without a hat, a horse without a rider, a house without a roof. We need our king and his wise counsel.

June 8, 1775

Verity came to me today when I was dusting Betsy's room and flung her arms around my middle. Laying her head against my chest, she sobbed and sobbed. She said she was tired of trying to be brave, that she wanted to go back home. I confess I cried with her, and it took us some time to calm down and wipe our faces.

Quickly, I took our golden star out of the small trunk

and held it up to my sister. She gasped and reached out for it. "That was a happy time, Pru." The light from the window shone through the gold paper, and for a moment, I felt peaceful.

June 12, 1775

I know not why I have taken so long to write. I feel dull and listless, in spite of all the noise and happenings outside. After church Papa took us down to see the troops marching in formation. They seem to be practicing for something, walking upright, shoulder to shoulder.

Betsy pointed, "There he is! Mr. Spaulding." We waved to him, Kate calling out his name. Mama hushed her, for we are not to disturb our troops when they are in formation.

Some men in plain clothes watched the troops and talked among themselves. They did not look happy, and Uncle Seth informed us that they were Patriots. Somehow I thought there would be more Tories in Boston than Patriots, but Uncle pointed to a group of them watching our soldiers and casting fierce looks at the red uniforms. Jacob has learned that some Patriots call them "bloody-backs." What a horrible and wicked name!

When I see soldiers marching, my stomach squeezes in, and my imagination makes terrible pictures inside. I see bullets slamming into soldiers' bodies. Blood flows over red uniforms. I hear the cries of sweethearts and family when they find their men have died in battle far from home.

I know not why such thoughts crowd my mind. Mama noticed my anxiety tonight and dosed me with chamomile tea, again. I do not think it will cure my fears.

June 14, 1775

Jacob has disappeared! Sometime after our noon-day meal, as we walked down to the wharves, Jacob slipped away from us, and we could not find him.

Papa says he shall have a whipping when he returns. Where can he be?

At night

Cousin Peter went looking for Jacob, and brought him back by the collar of his jacket at nine o'clock. We all were seated in the kitchen, talking worriedly of what might have happened.

"Jacob!" Papa strode forward and lifted him off the floor. "What happened to you?"

Jacob wiggled free and said, "I was trying to catch a fish, Papa, for I am dreadful tired of peas." He held up two shining silver fish. Somehow he had fashioned a line from Mama's thread and a bent pin.

Everyone cried out that we must have the fish now, this minute, and Phyllis gutted them, rolled them in cornmeal, and sizzled them in a pan over the fire. Even though there was only a mouthful for each of us, it cheered me to taste something fresh. It was like a sea breeze.

Kate laid down her fork and said, "Thank you, dear Jacob. Biddy likes fish." The doll nodded to show her approval, and we all went to bed. Is it not strange that Jacob was not punished, in spite of our worry?

June 15, 1775

I cannot write. Fear makes me tremble, like Verity in our bed at home. My stomach churns, my throat is choked, and I can tell no one why this is so. Is it my imagination or is it some other thing?

June 17, 1775

Somehow I must have known that danger lay ahead. This morning Papa heard a naval gun fired, and he and Uncle went out to get news. When they came back, they told us that the Patriots had marched out to Breed's Hill in the darkness and dug themselves into the top. When our troops found out, they took boats over, but the landing was delayed because of the tide. Now the battle is raging.

Aunt Dolly cried, "I wish to see this for myself!" We tucked some bread and cheese into our pockets and hurried off for the harbor, hoping to see something of the battle.

Cousin Betsy clutched my hand the whole way, saying, "Pray that Mr. Spaulding will be safe, Pru, pray hard!" So I did.

When we reached the wharves, there were crowds of people trying to see across the harbor. It was all noise, confusion, and the pounding roar of the cannons. I saw bursts of red flame, then black smoke bellied up from a place Uncle Seth called Charlestown. It looked as if the entire town were in flames.

It was too far away to follow the battle, even though the cannons kept booming across the bay. I pressed my hands to my ears, then put them over Kate's, for tears were rolling out of her eyes as she stood close to Mama.

The heat felt as if someone had opened the door to a huge bake oven. It blasted our faces, and the sun burned through my cap. We could only imagine how hot and weary our soldiers must be, carrying those heavy packs, trying to advance up the steep hill.

"It will be hard to dislodge the American forces at the top," Papa said, worried.

Uncle Seth and Cousin Peter shook their heads. "Never. They are too untrained to best us!" Papa kept his counsel, but Walter had persuaded him that the Patriots could be a formidable foe. Papa has learned that some of the seasoned soldiers from the French and Indian War are now commanding the militiamen.

Betsy fidgeted and fretted beside me. "Think you that Mr. Spaulding will be safe, Papa? Think you?"

He could not reassure her, and only answered that he hoped so. Finally, as Verity slumped against me, and Kate and Alice wailed from fatigue, we went back to Uncle Seth's house. Papa, Cousin Peter, Jacob, and Uncle Seth stayed on the wharves.

Tomorrow we shall know the outcome of this battle, one that Papa says is the first real one of this war. He calls Lexington and Concord "skirmishes."

War! I remember practicing that word in this very journal so many months ago. Now it is here.

Late at night

My hand trembles as I write this. None of us could sleep for the sound of carriage wheels rumbling along the lanes. Betsy and I crept downstairs to ask Papa what was happening, and he and Cousin Peter were dressed to go out at ten o'clock!

When we asked him what was happening, he told us Uncle Seth was bringing round his coach, and they would go out to Bunker Hill to pick up the British dead. Papa had heard there were many.

Aunt Dolly said fiercely, "We cannot leave them there!" Betsy clutched her mama's arm, wondering if Mr. Spaulding was safe. Did she think he was safe, did she? Cousin Peter ruffled her hair and told her that he would make inquiries about him.

We stood in the doorway, watching the coach disappear around a corner. Betsy clutched my hand and whispered, "After tonight, I shall never ride in Papa's coach again, never!"

June 18, 1775

At last our family is home, weary, sweat-stained, with reddened eyes. All night they went back and forth, gathering up the poor bodies and taking them to a place to be buried.

"At least they will be decently buried, Dolly," Mama said at dinner today.

Verity clutched my hand under the table. All I could think of was those young men, staring sightlessly into the dirt over their heads. I burst into tears and had to leave the table.

But before I left, Papa told us there were many more British soldiers dead than American soldiers, and that even though General Howe took the hill and the Patriots had to retreat, it was not a true victory. This is what I wish to know: *Who counts the dead?*

When Cousin Betsy kissed me good night, she said, "I cannot bear it, Pru! There is no news of my Nicholas." Indeed, her cheeks were hollow, and she clasped and unclasped her hands the way I remember a madwoman in Green Marsh did. I pray that her soldier is alive.

June 19, 1775

A great happiness today! After church Mr. Spaulding appeared at our door, exhausted, with one long red welt across his left cheek. With a cry, Betsy flung herself into his arms and sobbed, "I thought you were dead, Nicholas, I thought you were dead!"

Aunt Dolly firmed her lips, drew her daughter back inside, and told her not to make a spectacle of herself. I think Betsy cares not about being a spectacle.

Aunt seated Mr. Spaulding at the table and bade him join us for supper, which he did. He ate in wolfish bites, as if he had not fed in days. He told us that the battle was a disaster, a cruel disaster. When Papa asked why, he answered:

"General Howe is not a good general, sir! He let the Patriots get dug into Breed's Hill that night. He marched us up the hill the next day all in a line. They picked us off like crows, sir!" He slammed his glass down on the table.

No one said anything. He told us how they had twice advanced up the hill, losing hundreds of men on each charge. Then General Howe told the soldiers to take off their packs and form a bayonet charge. "I was glad of that!" Mr. Spaulding said.

"Then we had a chance," he said, sighing, and sat back in his chair. He told us that then the American soldiers retreated, for they had run out of bullets and only had stones to throw. But General Howe did not follow them. "Is that the way an army should be run, sir?" he asked Uncle Seth.

Betsy held his hand and sobbed quietly. It sent a chill through my body to think of our poor British soldiers being killed in a rain of bullets. Mr. Spaulding said that there were more British corpses on the ground than dead militiamen. "Far more."

Papa said this does not bode well for the war. Uncle Seth was silent. He has learned that the Patriots can and will fight like real soldiers.

June 21, 1775

Whenever Mr. Spaulding can take time away from his duties, he comes here. We discovered that he had received another wound in his shoulder, and Aunt Dolly bathes it whenever he arrives. She also feeds him any food we have. Mama is making sage tea to keep him healthy, for sometimes soldiers develop fevers from their wounds. It does her good to care for someone. She bustles about, gathering some of the herbs she brought with her, and making brews and tinctures. Truly, if women were allowed to be doctors, I think Mama would have been one.

Aunt Dolly and Uncle Seth seem to accept that Mr. Spaulding is courting Betsy. She seems less flighty now, and more serious. Perhaps the prospect of losing "her soldier" has sobered her.

Kate likes Mr. Spaulding and allowed him the great favor of holding Biddy on his lap this evening. He sang a song to the doll and clapped her small wooden hands together. Oh, I hope he shall be safe.

June 24, 1775

Papa and Uncle Seth continue to talk about the battles at Breed's Hill and Bunker Hill. Papa worries about the new commander of the American army, General George Washington, who has experience in battle. Uncle has drawn a map of Breed's Hill on a piece of foolscap, showing where the British forces advanced, and where the American forces were dug in.

According to Mr. Spaulding, the militiamen hid behind a long fence and then opened with murderous fire on our troops. They hide and dart and run like wolves.

How can our men in heavy uniforms, marching in formation side by side, fight against that?

Jacob has taken to wearing his winter coat and Papa's hat, pretending he is a soldier. With his sharpened stick against his shoulder, he walks back and forth across the yard in back. I tell him he is guarding the seedlings, and that is important.

June 27, 1775

I am tired of writing about war and death and disease and wounds and sadness. I took out our gold paper star and hung it over the bed I share with Betsy. A small breeze from the open window made it turn and glow, and it gave me hope that somehow things will get better, that we will celebrate Christmas once again in a house filled with pine boughs, good cheer, and family.

When Betsy came into our room before supper, she stopped and stared. "Oh, how beautiful!" she said, sitting beside me. The breeze stopped, the star became still, and we held our breath, as if somehow good fortune and the safety of our loved ones were held in that golden shape.

July 1, 1775

Today Mr. Spaulding came for supper. When he arrived, his cheeks had a hectic flush, yet he complained of the cold. Mama gave Papa a worried look, and went into the kitchen to brew him some sage tea. She kept Alice close by, not letting her wander over to Mr. Spaulding's side of the table during the meal.

After sipping the tea, Mr. Spaulding seemed a little better, and after supper, Betsy sang us a new song she had learned, which made us laugh, although Madame Pinprick would probably have called it *coarse.* How can words be coarse, like rough wool?

Mr. Spaulding bid us good night, and I noticed his uniform was not entirely clean. There were small brown spots all up and down the sleeves of his red military jacket. When I realized the spots were blood, I had to run outside into the street for some air, for my stomach was squeazy.

Papa says that even though war is not official yet, we are at war now. That word still makes me feel choked and breathless. How long will it go on? Will we ever go back home to Walter, to my room with the tiny maple desk, to Mama's stillroom, to our barn? I would even be happy to live with Madame Pinprick, if we could all be together again.

July 4, 1775

Bad news. A soldier came to tell us that Mr. Spaulding is ill. Betsy cried out that she would go visit him, but Mama told her in no uncertain terms that she was not to see Mr. Spaulding until he recovered. "I have seen those who visit the sick become ill themselves. That must not happen to you or to us."

My cousin set her lips in a mutinous look, scraped her shoe against the floor, but agreed. She does not wish to be sick any more than we do.

At night, Betsy would not come to bed but paced up and down in front of the window. It is so hot in this room! I thrust wide the window shutters, but there was no breeze, only the sad barking of dogs and someone crying out far away.

I wish we were someplace else on this earth.

July 5, 1775

Betsy sat on the stairs most of the day with her chin in her hand. All she talked of was her soldier; all she wished was to see him and bring him Mama's teas. "How else will he recover, Pru?"

She wanted to send their servant, Phyllis, off with some herbal brew, but Mama forbade it. She says we must wait until he is well. We hear news that some other soldiers have fallen sick, too. Mama hopes it is not the smallpox.

Smallpox! The very word makes my eyes squeeze shut. If we are no longer safe here, where *will* we be safe?

Jacob crept into our room tonight, before I doused the candle. He stood silent by my side, putting one hand on my shoulder. I do not know if he meant to comfort *me,* or if he wished me to comfort *him.* I gave him a long hug, but he said not a word.

July 7, 1775

Something is in the wind, but I am not sure what. This house buzzes like a beehive before the queen sets off to find a new nest. Mama rushes up and down stairs;

Papa follows her, asking questions, saying, "Martha, it will be all right. I promise you." She turned and said quickly, "I should be glad, Edward, glad!"

But what would she be glad of, and why was Papa reassuring her that it would be all right?

Later

Betsy stopped sitting on the stairs, as anxious as all of us to find out what is in the wind. We told her how the children of the family used to meet under our stairs back home, and we decided to do the same here.

Jacob, Verity, Kate, Betsy, and I huddled in that hot and crowded space to talk. Cousin Peter is too big and too old to be part of this gathering, and Alice is, of course, too little.

"I shall call this meeting to order!" Betsy rapped her knuckles against the floor. She said the first order of business was to find out what is happening, and she asked for volunteers.

Jacob thrust up his hand and offered to listen at closed doors, to walk along the city streets, and to gather up news. It is easier for a boy to dart about the streets than it is for us.

Then Kate rapped her knuckles against the floor and said, "We must keep Biddy safe. She must not get sick." She began to weep, and I had to cuddle and reassure her that Biddy should not fall ill, nor should we. At the same time, my sister held Biddy on *her* lap, cuddling her and whispering that she would protect her.

Betsy said that we would meet again to share our news.

July 10, 1775

Today the sad tidings reached us that Mr. Spaulding had died, along with a number of his companions. Mama thinks that a soldier's wounds can lead to fevers and disease. Betsy disappeared into our room, shutting the door, and she did not even come out for supper.

Kate asks where Mr. Spaulding is and seems not to believe that he is dead and will never come again. At tea, Uncle Seth bowed his head, and we all said a prayer for Betsy's soldier.

I wonder if there will be a funeral, and if we shall attend it? Poor Mr. Spaulding with his too-big hat and his gentle, kind manner. He deserved something better than a war in a foreign land and sudden death. Who will tell his mother and sisters what has befallen him?

July 11, 1775

Papa wears a frown on his face the day long. Mama snaps at Alice and is impatient with Verity and me. Worry hovers over us like the flies that come in through the open door. Betsy's face is red and swollen, and her lips look bruised. I do think she truly loved her soldier.

Betsy begged Uncle to find out where Nicholas was being buried, and he left the house to learn what he could. He returned several hours later, tired and bedraggled, with no news. "I could not find his regiment, and no one seemed to know, sweetheart."

This sent her upstairs in a fresh torrent of weeping. Poor Cousin Betsy! Even our Christmas star turning over the bed could not cheer her.

July 13, 1775

In spite of Betsy's sorrow, she called us to another meeting under the stairs, although it was hard to stay there for long due to the heat. Aunt has the back and front doors open, but all that comes in are dust and flies and no breeze at all. The air smells like a barn that has not been mucked out.

Jacob asked to speak. "I have no real news. Some soldiers have died, and they fear it is the smallpox." He went on to say that he stayed up late last night, camped outside Mama and Papa's door. He heard them talking of different places we could go to escape the hunger in Boston and the prospect of disease. They spoke of Nova Scotia, Bermuda, the West Indies, going west to land outside the colonies, but only one word came up again and again — Nantucket.

"Nantucket? Is that not an island?" Betsy exclaimed. "I would not live on an island for anything! We should be surrounded by water, storms, and waves!" She wrapped her arms around herself.

But my heart leaped like a boat catching the wind in its sails; Nantucket. It does have a goodly sound, and I believe no sickness would bother us there with all those fresh sea breezes.

July 15, 1775

We have had a conference at the table this morning, while we ate scones (no butter) and the last of Mama's raspberry preserves. Papa explained that he wanted to take us all to a safe place, away from Boston. Uncle and Aunt looked distressed and angry at the same time.

Uncle hated to leave his business and the safety of General Gage.

Mama said firmly that there *was* no safety here. Papa knows Seth's business is almost failing. Since they both have some savings, Papa wondered if they could invest in a business on Nantucket, for did not Seth have a distant cousin there?

Uncle paused and sucked in some smoke from his pipe. "We could wait out the war there and then decide what to do when it is all over," he said. Cousin Peter smoked, coughed, and when he got his breath he agreed that was a wise idea.

"When it is over," Aunt Dolly said, and sighed. Then she protested that Nantucket had many Quakers, and would they welcome us?

"Quakers have always been devoted to peace," Papa replied. "That is one reason I think it a goodly place." I wondered if there we might, once again, love our neighbors, and they would love us.

Jacob whispered the word "Nantucket, Nantucket," under his breath, tapping his fingers on the table. I crept away and went up to our room. Verity ran after to comfort me, but I was not sad. I squeezed Verity hard about the middle and told her I was *glad* we were going. There is no safety in Boston, and no safety back home.

It is time to leave. Besides, this quill is almost worn out. I can find a new quill on an island where geese come for safe harbor. Maybe it will be our safe harbor as well.

July 18, 1775

This is written in haste and sweat, surrounded by flies and pestered by cranky Alice. I do not like the way she looks with her flushed cheeks. Mama hopes it is teething, but she dosed her with sage tea this morning.

Phyllis and Guy, Aunt and Uncle's servants, are going home to their families, for they do not wish to sail to Nantucket. Uncle and Aunt shall have to get used to doing more of the work themselves.

My few dresses and corsets (could I not throw them into the sea?) are packed, and this book shall go in the midst of my sack with the Christmas star tucked between its pages for safekeeping.

Most of us are ready to go, all except my cousin, who cannot decide what dresses to bring. Papa reminded us that we could only take one cloth sack with our most precious possessions. Jacob takes his new coat from the linsey-woolsey given to Mama as payment for a birth.

Kate begged to borrow one of my handkerchiefs to

tie around Biddy's yarn hair, "for Papa says it shall be blowy on the ship."

Papa and Uncle said at dinner that they had a deal of trouble finding a boat to take us across the harbor. You cannot sail directly to Nantucket Island because of the shoals, so we have to go to Cape Cod first. They had to pay extra money to a fisherman with a two-masted boat. Jacob tells me the front is called the "bow" and the back is called the "stern." Ever since he has learned we are sailing, he has spent every moment he can snatch by the wharves, learning about boats.

Two days from hence, we leave at night.

July 20, 1775

This is our last evening in Uncle Seth's house. We ate porridge at the table, but Jacob could not stay in his seat, no matter how often Aunt and Mama chided him. Kate sat beside me holding Biddy and spooning food up to her small cloth mouth. Alice, who is no longer flushed, had a cup of grown-up tea and crowed with delight. "Big girl!" she announced.

Verity's face was pale as a bleached sheet, for she fears the coming sea voyage. Only Peter, Uncle Seth, and I seem to be looking forward to this journey. Papa does not trust the sea, but he says that he trusts not the land, either, for it is full of war, treason, blood, and intemperate men. He said that we shall have to be very careful when we leave before dawn tomorrow. No one is allowed to leave Boston harbor, and even though we are loyal to the king, the British soldiers might try to stop us.

Later

As I wrote my last entry in this house, Betsy told me her nerves are stretched to breaking. She whirled about the room, packing this, discarding that. She muttered under her breath, "An island, an island far away," and cried a little. With my help she finally stuffed her dresses, underthings, and corsets into a sack, still crying.

Verity came in for a kiss before going to bed with Kate. In a small voice she asked if we should be safe on the voyage over? Carefully, I took the gold star from between the pages of this book and held it up. "This shall protect us," I told her, "and God."

She went back to her room to sleep, no longer afraid.

July 22, 1775, written behind a coil of rope as our boat rides in harbor

We are away from Boston! We left yesterday on the tide, well before the sun came up.

Mama shook us awake in the darkness, and we met downstairs. Papa divided us into three groups for safety: He led one, Uncle Seth the other, and Cousin Peter the last. We carried our sacks with us, food, and rolled-up blankets to use on board.

There were few soldiers patrolling at that time of night, and we were careful to keep out of their sight. We crept to a little used wharf, where our boat awaited us, climbed aboard, stowed our sacks, and were allowed to sit at the back. It is a working boat, not too big. There was one other family fleeing Boston for Nantucket, but we did not talk to them right away. I could dimly make out a girl sitting with her face to the wind, and I thought that a good sign.

The owner gave a command, the two sails were run up, and a sailor untied the rope holding us to the wharf. The sound of the wind bellying out the sails made my heart leap. Oh, the ink just splattered. It is difficult writing on my lap, with my precious bottle of ink on the deck before me. Kate is holding it still for me.

We sailed out into the darkness, avoiding the huge British men-of-war. A thin moon gave us some light to see by, but not so much as to be dangerous. My family huddled together behind the rope; Papa held Alice on his lap, while Mama snuggled with Verity and Jacob. I could see my uncle with his arm around my aunt, and as the boat left harbor, Betsy called softly, "Good-bye, Nicholas, good-bye."

I hugged Kate and told her not to be afraid, that we would reach Nantucket safely and make a new home there. Perhaps one day we would hang up our golden star and celebrate Christmas.

Surprised, she said, "But Pru, I am not afraid." Then she held Biddy up in the fresh salty wind and said, "See how dark it is, Biddy? Soon the sun will rise and we will sail over the water like birds flying."

So my six-year-old sister gave us words for a safe passage.

Epilogue

Nantucket did not turn out to be the safe harbor that Papa and Uncle Seth had hoped for. But in spite of many hardships, Prudence's family managed to make their home there. Uncle Seth and Papa had enough money to invest in some whaling ships. Although some whalers were captured by the British, Papa and Uncle Seth's ships remained safe, and soon they earned enough money to build a house on the edge of town.

Mama continued to be a midwife and became a beloved figure on the island. The islanders used to say that Mrs. Emerson never lost a baby or a mother.

Jacob grew up to be a carpenter's apprentice, who took joy in pounding nails and seeing boards become houses and furniture. Although he and his sisters loved celebrations, they could never bear to attend the Fourth of July parties when fireworks were set off. The memories of the battle at Breed's Hill and the sound of cannons never quite left them.

Verity was apprenticed to a seamstress after the war and was much in demand. As she used to tell Prudence, "Sewing does not call for bravery, and so it suits me well."

Kate stayed at home with Mama and Papa. With her sensitive fingers, sharp nose, and love of plants, she created one of the finest herb gardens on Nantucket. No one ever knew that until the end of her life, Kate slept beside a doll with delicately carved fingers and toes, who wore a faded yellow dress.

Walter stayed in Green Marsh, farming and running the store. At the end of the war he wrote often, asking the family to come back, but Papa refused to return to the village that had rejected him. Eventually, Walter married Abigail Owens and became a leading figure in the village. Perhaps he had always been a Patriot in his heart after all, and no one but Prudence ever suspected his secret.

Walter's letters told of the Pratt family simply disappearing one night, and no one ever heard of them again. Papa supposed they had fled to some safer part of the country.

Uncle Seth's family did not flourish on Nantucket. Aunt Dolly said the air was too thin and did not agree with her. Betsy would have no one for a husband but a British soldier, and Cousin Peter had always yearned to join the British army. After the war ended, they sailed to England, making a home in Surrey.

Prudence became friends with Ruth Hawthorne, the girl who had fled Boston on the same boat. Through her, she met Ruth's brother, Charles, who worked as a ship builder. When peace came, Pru married Charles, and they set up house within sight of the sea. They had five children, all of them safely delivered by Mama.

Prudence lived longer than anyone else in her family, with the exception of Alice, who married a Quaker. After Charles, Mama, and Papa died, Kate came to live with Prudence. Often Kate, Pru, and Alice would sit on the gray porch of the island house, listening to the far sound of the breakers against the shore. When Pru asked them if they remembered Green Marsh, her two sisters would shake their heads and smile. "No," Kate and Alice would answer. "No, not at all."

But Prudence remembered the solemn bonging of the grandfather clock, the loss of her old friend Abigail, and a boy with red hair who might have been a fine friend, had he only been a Tory or she, a Patriot.

Historical Note

Who were the Tories? Were they people like you and me who had somehow made the decision to support the "wrong" side in the American Revolution?

History books say very little about Tories, and what they do say is never terribly complimentary. The myth has grown up over the years that Tories — or Loyalists, as they sometimes called themselves — were always rich people. That myth also says they supported the king of England because they wanted to protect their wealth and the old ways.

Although that may have been true for some, many Tories were people like you and me, everyday people leading everyday lives. They might have been bricklayers, farmers, small-shop owners, merchants, fishermen, cobblers, pewter makers, or any other occupation a colonist might have had.

In general, Tories were the conservatives of their day, in the years leading up to 1774, the start of this fictional diary set in the fictional town of Green Marsh.

They wished to preserve the established government with allegiance to Britain and its king. They saw King George as their leader appointed by God; to be a Tory was to support the natural order of things. To be a Patriot was to tear down that order.

The best estimates are that Tories made up about 33 percent of the population in the thirteen colonies. Life became immeasurably difficult for them in the fall of 1774. The history leading up to the Revolution reads like an account of an angry father trying to discipline his rebellious children. King George, and many in Parliament, never could recognize the rights of the colonies and their wish to govern themselves.

Going back to the 1760s, Britain passed several acts that influenced the history of our story. The "Stamp Act," for example, fixed a tax on all sorts of papers, from legal documents and letters to newspapers and almanacs. They also passed a law that forced American towns and cities to "quarter" (house) British troops and feed them.

At the Boston Tea Party, in December 1773, Patriots (and merchants) angry at British taxation of tea dumped many chests of tea into Boston Harbor. In retaliation, an angry Britain passed a series of resolutions that the colonists called the "Intolerable Acts." These closed the Port of Boston until the money lost over the dumped tea was repaid; they put General Gage in charge of the government of Massachusetts, sending more than ten thousand troops to keep order; and these acts took away the charter of the Colony of Massachusetts, which had allowed citizens a measure of self-government. The "Intolerable Acts" were printed on broadsides, sent around Massachusetts, and often burned in bonfires by angry Patriots.

Persecution of the Tories began to increase in the fall of 1774, when this diary begins. When the "Suffolk Resolves" were passed by Patriots in Boston, they helped set the stage for the Revolution by declaring that they would organize their own militias; they would form their own government, independent of the king; and they would not trade with Britain. On a wider canvas, the First and Second Continental Congresses, which met in Philadelphia, gathered men from all the colonies to respond to Britain. Their task was to figure out how to preserve their rights without actually separating from England. But as time passed, it became clear that the colonies must separate and form their own government. That was officially sealed in the Declaration of Independence, written in the summer of 1776, after the end of this diary.

After the battle of Lexington and Concord, the persecution against Tories increased. Some men had balls of tar and feathers delivered to them, signaling that they would be tarred and feathered, and they ran out of town. Many Tory properties were confiscated by Patriots and kept, never to be returned, even after the war.

Many Tories fled to Boston for the protection of General Gage, only to find, like Prudence's family, that Boston suffered from a lack of supplies. After a series of military disasters by their army, the British were finally persuaded to depart from Boston. On March 17, 1776, a huge flotilla of ships set sail from the harbor. There were about 1,100 Tories on those boats, along with their belongings and some animals, who sailed north to Nova Scotia to make a home. It was a hard place to settle, and during the first winter many lived in tents and suffered from cold, hunger, and sickness. The Tories called their new country "Nova Scarcity."

Other Loyalists fled to the Bahamas, Bermuda, farther west in America, and sometimes farther south. Some stayed put, keeping their heads down and hoping to survive the Revolution relatively unnoticed. One estimate is that around 100,000 Tories left the colonies during the War of Independence.

We often fail to realize that the American Revolution

was also a civil war: it pitted part of a town against another part; it set parents against their children. Benjamin Franklin had an illegitimate son who was a Tory of high position. Obviously, they did not agree on the course America should follow. It wasn't just a fight to separate from Britain, it was also a struggle that deeply split this country. And, like all such wars, it took generations to heal.

Hatred against Tories persisted well into the 1800s, and laws against them on the books often did not disappear until after the War of 1812.

Of course Tories were not always victims, nor did they always act innocently. They had their part in resisting the Revolution, the new government, and laws passed by Patriots. They supported the British army, to the dismay of the Patriots. But it is important to see the other side of the story; to remind ourselves that men, women, and children of good intent, living everyday lives, suffered greatly — and sometimes unjustly — during this war.

What would you have done had you been alive in 1774? Which side would you have been on?

A New England farmhouse.

A colonial American family prepares to make soap by boiling lard and other ingredients that may give the soap a pleasing aroma and texture.

Angry Patriots and merchants, infuriated by the British crown's decision to tax the American colonies' imported tea, dumped many chests of tea into Boston Harbor in December 1773. This became known as the Boston Tea Party, and King George III then closed the Port of Boston until the cost of the tea was recouped.

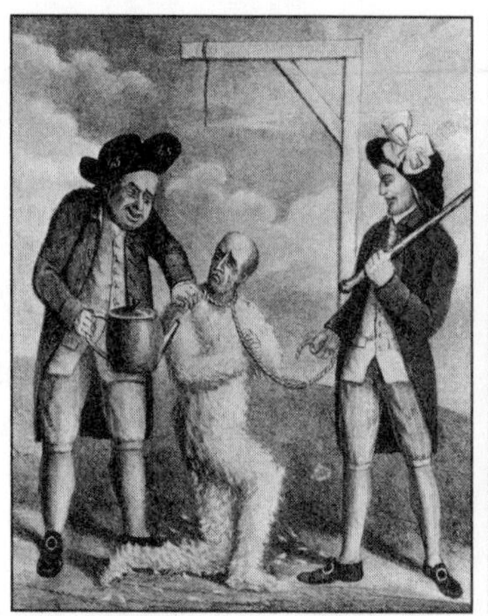

After the Boston Tea Party, Tories, or Loyalists, became the targets of harsh and cruel treatment in the colonies. Some Patriots even resorted to tar and feathering (left), *and many Tories had difficulty leading normal lives in their communities with Patriot neighbors.*

Citizens watch the battle at Breed's and Bunker Hill taking place across Boston Harbor.

Many Tory families fled Boston due to the scarcity of supplies and food and because they feared for their lives. A few escaped by ship to Nantucket, where they made their new homes.

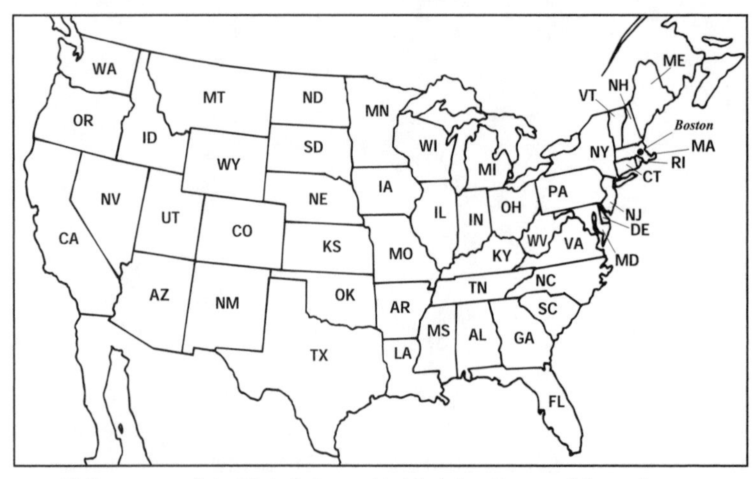

Modern map of the United States highlighting Boston, Massachusetts.

About the Author

What would it have been like to be a Tory in the year leading up to the American Revolution? Are there any connections between a thirteen-year-old girl of 1774 and someone of today? These are questions I asked myself when I set out to write a fictional diary of Prudence Emerson, who never is and never was "prudent."

I had Tories on my mother's side of the family history, as well as Patriots. When I found out I had Tories in my family, I felt betrayed, as if my people had supported the wrong side in the Revolution. For on my dad's side, the Warrens, we claimed an ancient link with Joseph Warren, the famous radical doctor in Boston who did so much to shape the Revolution in Massachusetts and who was killed in the Battle of Bunker Hill.

But the more research I did, the more I came to realize that Tories were people, too, not just *enemies*. They had hopes, dreams, and aspirations, families and farms and communities. I wanted to get behind the mask of historical facts and find out what it was like to be a Tory girl in 1774.

What I found confirmed my fears: It would have been a difficult and hard time to be alive, particularly in Massachusetts, where persecution of and laws against Tories were harsher than in some other colonies.

I wanted to explore how a girl survived a sad time, when what she had known and loved was taken away from her. What were her strengths, and how did she keep going through such hard times?

When you think about these questions, you are making historical connections. You are thinking about the ways in which girls of more than two hundred years ago survived hard times and how *you* endure difficult times today. I think many of the same qualities help us to win: patience (not my strong point), hope, love of family, humor, courage, faith, and celebrating rituals that give us a sense of the future — as putting up the Christmas star did for Pru's family.

She knew, as did her sister Kate, that a time would come when the sun would rise again, and they would "sail over the water like birds flying."

Ann Turner is the author of acclaimed historical fiction, including the picture books *Katie's Trunk* and *Abe Lincoln Remembers*, as well as the historical novels *Grasshopper Summer* and *Dear America: The Girl Who Chased Away Sorrow*. She lives with her family in Williamsburg, Massachusetts.

Acknowledgments

I want to give special thanks to the many people who helped me in my research for *Love Thy Neighbor:*

Mrs. Elise Feeley, Reference Librarian at Forbes Library, who went out of her way to get facts about schools for girls, language, the celebration of Christmas, and stage travel in 1774.

Ms. Ann Lanning, Associate Curator for Interpretation of Historic Deerfield, who graciously answered my many questions about details of everyday life and husbandry.

Ms. Susan McGowan, interpreter, and other staff at Historic Deerfield who conducted an open hearth cooking demonstration.

Ms. Frances Karttunen, from the Nantucket Historical Association Research Library Museum, who helped gather facts about boat travel during 1775 and the emigration of Tories to Nantucket.

Tom Kelleher, Research Historian, and Christie Higginbottom, Project Coordinator, at Old Sturbridge Village.

Cary Antil, friend, who gave me information about old apple varieties.

This book could not have been written without your help.

Grateful acknowledgment is made for permission to reprint the following:

Cover Portrait: *Marianne Becket,* by Anna C. Peale, courtesy of Historical Society of Pennsylvania Collection, Atwater Kent Museum.

Cover Background: *1775—The Battle of Lexington,* by Amos Doolittle, courtesy of the New York Public Library, Stokes Collection.

Page 181 (top): A New England farmhouse, Getty Images, Inc.

Page 181 (bottom): Making soap, Brown Brothers.

Page 182 (top): The Boston Tea Party, RG 148-Minor Congressional Committee, photo no. 148-GW-439 in the National Archives.

Page 182 (bottom, left): Tar and feathering, Bettmann/CORBIS.

Page 182 (bottom, right): Humiliating Tories, Culver Pictures.

Page 183: Citizens watch the battle at Breed's and Bunker Hill, Culver Pictures.

Page 184 (top): Nantucket wharf, courtesy of the Nantucket Historical Association.

Page 184 (bottom): Map by Heather Saunders.

Other Dear America and My Name Is America books about the Revolutionary War

The Winter of Red Snow
The Revolutionary War Diary of Abigail Jane Stewart
by Kristiana Gregory

The Journal of William Thomas Emerson
A Revolutionary War Patriot
by Barry Denenberg

Other Dear America books by Ann Turner

The Girl Who Chased Away Sorrow
The Diary of Sarah Nita, a Navajo Girl

This book is lovingly dedicated to my husband, Rick, and my two children, Ben and Charlotte. They endured with me while I wrote and revised and polished and sweated.

While the events described and some of the characters in this book may be based on actual historical events and real people, Prudence Emerson is a fictional character, created by the author, and her diary and its epilogue are works of fiction.

Library of Congress Cataloging-in-Publication Data
Turner, Ann Warren.
Love thy neighbor : the Tory diary of Prudence Emerson / by Ann Turner.
p. cm. — (Dear America)
Summary: In Green Marsh, Massachusetts, in 1774, thirteen-year-old Prudence keeps a diary of the troubles she and her family face as Tories surrounded by American Patriots at the start of the American Revolution.
ISBN 0-439-15308-5
1. United States — History — Revolution, 1775–1783 — Juvenile fiction. [1. United States — History — Revolution, 1775–1783 — Fiction. 2. American loyalists — Fiction. 3. Massachusetts — History — Colonial period, ca. 1600–1775 — Fiction. 4. Diaries — Fiction.] I. Title. II. Series.
PZ7.T8535 Lo 2003
[Fic] — dc21 2002073345

---

10 9 8 7 6 5 4 3 2 1 03 04 05 06 07

The display type was set in HoeflerText Italic.
The text type was set in Cochin.
Book design by Elizabeth B. Parisi
Photo research by Dwayne Howard and Amla Sanghvi

Printed in the U.S.A. 23
First edition, April 2003